MASSACRE AT
SALT CREEK

Also by Blaine M. Yorgason:

CHARLIE'S MONUMENT
THE WINDWALKER
OTHERS
(*co-authored with Brenton G. Yorgason*)

MASSACRE AT
SALT CREEK

BLAINE M. YORGASON

DOUBLEDAY & COMPANY, INC.
GARDEN CITY, NEW YORK
1979

First Edition

ISBN: 0-385-15200-0
Library of Congress Catalog Card Number 78–22744
Copyright © 1979 by Blaine M. Yorgason
All Rights Reserved
Printed in the United States of America

For Kathy,

who has the courage of the woman!

INTRODUCTION

On June 4, 1858, five Mormon pioneers, traveling unarmed on their way to Sanpete Valley, Utah Territory, were attacked in Salt Creek Canyon by a party of renegade Ute Indians. Four of the Mormons were massacred, while the fifth escaped unharmed.

In the years since then, many legends have grown out of this event, legends that may or may not have their basis in fact. Still, these legends continue to inspire the curious traveler to pause on his way through the lonely canyon of Salt Creek and read the tarnished brass plaque on the old monument erected in memory of the massacre.

DAUGHTERS OF THE UTAH PIONEERS NO. 11
Erected June 4, 1936
SALT CREEK CANYON MASSACRE

This monument replaces one previously erected (that crumbled through weather conditions) by Langley A. Bailey Sr., Jacob Bowers and Henry Knowles in memory of the following pioneers: Jens Jergensen and wife, Jens Terkelsen and Christian E. Kjerulf who were massacred by Indians June 4, 1858 near this spot while traveling unarmed on their way to Sanpete Valley.

As he reads he may wonder that there is no mention made of the fifth person, the one who escaped, or he may wonder that nowhere does it indicate that the woman had a name other than "wife." Finally he may wonder that four and perhaps more lives could be lived out in their entirety and then be brought to so sudden a conclusion with such a brief and unfeeling epitaph left to record their passing.

Then as he steps back he may note the stillness, the loneliness of the canyon. Not much has changed in the hundred and some years since the massacre occurred. The dusty valley, the churning and foaming creek, the rock-strewn hills, the brush-choked draws, and the hard-boned and wind-whipped ridges leading into the mysterious

darkness of the high-up timber all combine to give him the feeling
that the massacre might have happened yesterday instead of so long
ago.

It is, therefore, with a sense of relief that he climbs back into his
car and drives away from this place so haunted with unspoken memories.

The following story is an account of those memories. The names
used are, in the case of the Mormons, the actual names of the people
who played out that historical drama in Salt Creek Canyon so many
years ago. The personalities, however, have been developed in their
entirety by the author, and any resemblance to real people, either
living or dead, is entirely coincidental and must be considered as
such.

The Indians named, while probably not a part of the massacre,
were, with the exception of Hoskoots, real people who lived in Utah
Territory during that tumultuous period. All of them, and especially
Inepegut, were involved at one time or another with the Mormons.
Inepegut means crazy, and he was considered insane by his people.
He was also known as a killer by them and by the Mormons. At one
point, following one of his particularly brutal killings, a band of Utes
bound him and carried him three days into the Uinta Mountains
where they tied him, naked, to a lightning-blasted pine. Leaving him
there to die they rode furiously back to Utah Valley, not pausing
even for rest in their journey. Imagine their fear when, upon their arrival, they found Inepegut sitting naked on the bank of the stream
laughing insanely at them. From that point onward he was totally os-
tracized, and after that lived alone in a brush wickiup in the hills
above Santaquin.

The massacre occurred during the larger historical event known as
the Utah War, and was probably an indirect result of that conflict.
Weapons were scarce, and it seems likely that the massacred Mormons were unarmed simply because they had no choice. The militia,
known as the Nauvoo Legion, needed all the weapons it could get if
it was going to hold off the Army of the United States.

So the people's names and the major historical events portrayed in
the following account are historical. Other than that, the story is entirely fictional and should be regarded as such.

Blaine M. Yorgason

CHAPTER ONE

The silence of the afternoon was profound and deep. The canyon breeze, always brisk in the mornings, had slipped away, and there was no movement in the mountain swale, no movement at all. The long grass, thick and green with spring, stood still in the afternoon sun, and the quietness was so intense that a tiny lizard, its sides heaving in the heat, suddenly darted from its sun-shrouded rock and scurried beneath the protection of a fragrant clump of sage.

High overhead an old buzzard drifted silently across the swale, his shadow the only sign of his passing. His sharp old eyes missed nothing as the warm air whistled softly past his slightly tilted wingtips.

The old mortician of the mountains was in no hurry, for to him, time meant simply the distance from one meal to the next. Of course that distance always varied, yet he had learned from long experience that he could only allow it to vary so much before his most recent meal would become his final one. So he circled, always searching, waiting patiently for the time when his instincts told him it was time to feast.

Beneath the old buzzard, in the bottom of the swale, a muscular brown figure lay still as death midst the rocks and the grass, carefully eyeing the lazy sweeping circles of the old buzzard. The man's black eyes were narrowed against the glare of the afternoon sun, and his arms were stretched to the sides much as though he were bound to the earth.

And so he was, but not with stakes and cords of rawhide. No, the cords which bound him were cords of fear, of caution, of confusion, of insanity. For he was Inepegut, he was the Crazy Man of the Utes, he was the Killer! And that was why his tortured brain was struggling so awfully.

Why was he here? Why was it he who was on the ground, instead of that stupid oaf of a man, Hoskoots, the Ugly One, he whose face made a mockery of anything human? It was he who should be on the ground. On the ground and with the blade of Inepegut buried to the hilt in his chest.

Why . . . ?

With darting eyes the Crazy One again glanced at his weitch lying inches beyond his grasp, its bright blade gleaming in the sunlight. Why, with a quick movement and a little luck . . .

Inepegut was also aware of the silent, staring circle of onlookers squatting on the hills around the swale intently watching this mortal struggle, and the man Inepegut knew great shame as he pictured himself through their eyes, cowering in the o-coomp, the dust, at the feet of the Ugly One.

He could see Namowah, his black eyes dancing with laughter that his stern visage could not conceal. There also was Tutsegavit, a thin man who was making no effort at all to conceal his mirth. He could not see Ankawakeets, yet he knew that that giant, too, was smiling, as were many of the others in the circle. Inepegut hated them all with a vicious and unreasoning hatred that knew no bounds.

Again his eyes shifted, and now he could see Chipetz, her leather dress torn across her slender shoulder, her whole body wracked with sobs as she sat slumped just inside the circle of watching men.

Chipetz! Oh how Inepegut ached for that squaw. But now . . . And those others, they wanted her too. Pintus and, wonder of all wonders, Hoskoots, the Ugly One. Inepegut suddenly broke the silence with a loud cackle as he thought of the absurdity of the misshapen face of the Ugly One appealing to one with the beauty of Chipetz.

Again he cackled, lying there on the ground, and as he did so his eyes shifted back to Hoskoots, who stood, slightly stooping with his breath coming in ragged gasps, his own weitch gripped tightly in his massive right hand.

And as he laughed Inepegut noted that Hoskoots flinched and stepped back a little at the sudden sound, his eyes darting then in sudden shame toward Chipetz, hoping that she had not discerned his fear.

All this Inepegut saw, and he laughed aloud once again as he realized what it all meant, his laughter a high-pitched shrieking that caused shivers on the backs of those who heard him.

Squawpulling! That was how it had started.

Squawpulling. If two men wanted the same woman for a squaw, and if neither had sufficient wealth to sway the father of the squaw in his own favor, then the issue was decided by a squawpulling. The prospective bride would be placed in the center of a large circle and the two braves who wanted her as a wife would each take hold of one of her arms. The friends of the competing braves would then line up behind their respective leaders to form a human chain. Then a massive and desperate tug-of-war would ensue, the object of which was to pull the hapless squaw across one line or the other. The victor, of course, would have the squaw.

That is, he would have her if she lived through the ordeal and managed meanwhile to keep both arms securely attached to her body.

Wagh! How many squawpullings had Inepegut seen? He had no idea, but it was many. So why had he gone berserk when he had come over the hill and had seen this one? Without thinking or even planning he had thrown himself upon the younger but much larger Hoskoots, there had been a brief and desperate flurry of struggling bodies and flashing knives, and suddenly he had found himself in his present situation, disarmed and flat on his back.

Oo-ah, he should be dead! But Hoskoots was katz-te-suah, he was foolish. There he stood, his eyes wide and the smell of fear all over him, holding back when he should have been attacking.

Suddenly Inepegut was so angry that it was he on the ground instead of the foolish Hoskoots that he broke into tears, and at this Hoskoots took another step back, his fear of the insane overcoming his pride and desire to destroy this killer, this Inepegut.

Without warning Inepegut grabbed a handful of dust and pebbles and with a sweeping motion threw them at Hoskoots while he at the same instant rolled over, swept up his weitch, and leaped to his feet.

It was an old trick, very old, and Hoskoots had almost been expecting it.

Almost.

A little late he saw the dirt and gravel coming, and in ducking a stone rolled under his foot and he lost his balance. And that alone saved his life.

Had he been erect the sweeping blade of Inepegut would have dispatched him easily. As it was he received a deep gash across his shoulder, while the momentum of Inepegut carried him across the still falling body of Hoskoots and down again into the rocks and the brush.

Another inglorious defeat was more than the crazed mind of

Inepegut could handle. With a terrible shriek he leaped to his feet and began to bound up and down, and then to the wonderment and fear of Hoskoots and all those present the Crazy One, the Killer, threw his knife to the earth and sprinted up the hill to a large cedar which he quickly climbed. There in the uppermost branches he gave vent to the grief and frustration of the moment, tearing at the air with loud moans and wails.

Hesitantly Hoskoots notched an arrow to his bow, wanting and yet fearing to end this battle permanently, for who knew what powers such a crazy man might have.

Suddenly old Tackwitch the medicine man, the wrinkled and wise one, held up his hand, and Hoskoots instantly lowered his bow.

"No, Ugly One. God, the Great To-Wats, has forbidden that we slay the Crazy One, or any others like him. Ignore him. Let him go his way. To all of us it must be as though he is already dead, for with his mind it is truly so."

Now Tackwitch rose slowly to his feet and shuffled over to the still sobbing Chipetz, the young woman who had been the center of the recently interrupted squawpull.

Roughly he jerked her to her feet, and at the grimace of pain on her face Hoskoots almost attacked the old man.

Almost!

But he didn't, for he knew the power of the old myshoot-te towats, and he wanted nothing to do with that awful power.

"Pintus! Hoskoots! Men of the People! There will be no more squawpulling this day, or any other day for this squaw! She will return to the wickiup of her father and remain there until one or the other of you comes with enough to purchase her fairly."

Suddenly he grinned a toothless grin and roughly squeezed her arm.

"Oo-ah, but this little squaw is a fine one. Oo-ah, yes, she should be worth much!"

At that the whole crowd broke into laughter and began to file out of the swale. In a moment only Hoskoots and Pintus remained.

"Wagh, Ugly One," snarled Pintus, shaking his fist at Hoskoots. "Would that I instead of the Crazy One had held his blade. If so, this matter would even now be decided.

"Still, within hours I will have the wealth and therefore the squaw. So go, Ugly One! Hide your face in the kibah, for only the mountains can stomach your ugliness."

With that he turned his back upon the angry but irresolute Hoskoots and strode disdainfully out of the swale.

Hoskoots stood still only a moment longer before he too climbed out of the draw, and he ignored totally the threats of death screamed at him by the treed Inepegut, for Tackwitch himself said that it must be as though the Crazy One were already e-i, already dead.

Besides, he had more important things to think about now. Things that were much more important.

Somewhere in these mountains he would find wealth. And when he found it, he would obtain that for which he had been born. Ooah, but he was certain of it.

CHAPTER TWO

The sun was more than three hours high when the woman first saw the dust in the air. It was not really dust, rather more just a suggestion of it that she saw. Shivering, she pulled her shawl more tightly about her shoulders, adjusted her position on the wagon seat, and glanced back beyond the canvas into the wagon box. She did this continually, and yet each observation added a new sense of wonder to her sorrow and bitterness. For lurch, jolt, and bounce as the wagon did, the baby managed to sleep peacefully through it all, snug in the box Jens had secured to the side of the wagon. How could anyone, even a tiny baby, sleep through the misery of the journey into this God-forsaken canyon?

The wagon lurched again as it slid over a large boulder worn smooth by countless years of running water, and as the woman clutched the seat to maintain her balance she allowed her eyes to scan the hills around them. She had done this constantly since their journey had begun, and though she could describe with amazing accuracy all the country they had passed through, she looked not so much for what she could see, the obvious, as she did for that which was out of place, the unordinary. This was a natural habit that had been born during the twenty years she had spent growing up on the frontier.

She thought then of her father, quiet, stern, fierce when riled (which was often), competent in situations where lesser men would have been helpless. As a young girl she had learned from him how to track, to follow a trail not merely by hoof- and footprint but also by slight and subtle disturbances, such as crushed grass, an overturned or scraped pebble or stone, freshly broken twigs or leaves, and so on. It was, he explained over and over to her, simple observation that kept some men alive while others perished. Always look for that which is not exactly as it should be, he would say, and most always a body will be able to handle whatever occurs.

And she wondered now, as she thought of his instructions, how he would handle the desperate situation in which she now found herself. Would he stay and make the best of a bad deal, as he used to say, or would he simply . . . ?

There! Up on top of that ridge! Yes, it was dust! The woman was certain of it. Not heavy, though, just a faint haze in the air that might have passed unnoticed, except that the woman knew exactly what she was looking for and even almost exactly where to look for it.

One rider, at the most two, had been on that ridge not more than ten minutes before. That meant they had either seen or at least heard the wagon. It also meant, and she was almost afraid to think this thought, that whoever it was did not want to be seen.

Of course the woman forced herself to admit that not wishing to be seen was not necessarily evil. On the trail some folks just naturally made a wide berth of others in order to avoid sharing their problems.

Here in Utah Territory, though, where most everyone was a Mormon, the reverse was usually true. It might possibly be U.S. soldiers, but she doubted it. They were all up in Echo Canyon, and there was little likelihood any of them would be this far south. Still it was a possibility, so she worried. Why, she didn't know exactly, but she did feel worried and so cast her eyes upon the hills around her constantly.

She considered for a moment telling the men of her suspicions, but quickly discarded the idea. Even if they believed her, and she doubted they would, they would still be powerless to do anything about it. Especially considering the kind of men they were.

Especially then!

Another heavy jolt brought the woman's attention back once again to the sleeping infant, and as she gazed at its tiny features she found it was all she could do to keep from bursting into tears.

Why did it have to be her? Why was she being forced through all this agony once more?

Four brothers she had seen die as babies, four brothers and a mother, and all of them going after she had prayed so hard for God to let them stay. Then add to that her own child, a beautiful little boy that she felt certain would live to become the means whereby she could at last draw truly close to her husband.

But no, three hours was all God had given her with her little son before he too was dead. Three hours! Where was the divine justice in that, she wondered? Especially when she had prayed so hard and had needed that child so badly. Couldn't God see that?

Again she looked at the baby in the box, thinking of the hours of silent grief old Jens had endured as he sat by her side following the baby's death. He was a good man, and she knew he was. If he only wasn't so bumbling and so helpless and so confounded willing to be pushed around by anyone who wanted to push him around. It was almost as though he had no will of his own, and though she knew that deep down she almost loved him, she still found herself hating him for his spinelessness, his inability to act as a man truly should act.

The baby started squirming, and as the woman looked at it again, tiny, helpless, little eyes squinted tightly against the light, hands bunched into miniature fists, she suddenly knew that this child too would die. It would die in spite of Jens's professed faith that it would live to give him posterity, a faith in divine inspiration which he staunchly claimed that he had received.

"Ja," she could hear him say, "the Lord has promised, und I know it vill be true. Ve vill have posterity from this child." Oh if he could only know, if he could understand as she understood. This baby girl could not live, and she no doubt would be forced to watch it die in some dirt-floored cabin somewhere in this miserable desolate wilderness of Sanpete Valley. In a way she even hated the child for the anguish she knew it would bring her, and she felt trapped and helpless, with no place to go to escape the misery that she knew was coming.

Polygamy! How she was coming to loathe the thought of eternal plural marriage! Why had she done it? Why had she gone along with her father's desire that she become the plural wife of this weak old man, this Jens Jergensen? Certainly she had cared for him and did even now, to some extent. But glory, he was older than her own father had been when he had died. It was just crazy, that was what it was!

Trouble was, at the time of the marriage she had readily agreed. It had, in fact, all seemed very logical. Though she didn't know Jens Jergensen very well, she was awfully close to Kjersta, his wife. Kjersta had been like a mother and big sister all rolled into one since her own mother had died, and when her father had been critically injured while cutting logs for a new cabin he had naturally felt concerned about his daughter's future. So, he had called Jens and Kjersta to him and suggested that his daughter become the plural wife of old Jens.

Kjersta had readily agreed to the idea. Jens, seeing that his wife made no objections, simply said, "Ja, I vill do it, old friend," and that was that. Two weeks later, one week after her father's death, the woman had been sealed to Jens Jergensen as a plural wife by Heber C. Kimball, counselor to President Brigham Young.

The woman almost grinned as she recalled how excited Jens and Kjersta had been. They had been married nearly twenty years but had not been blessed with children, and now they were convinced that the Lord was about to bless their family with posterity.

Again the woman's eyes swept the hills around them as she lifted the shawl to screen out the choking dust the oxen and wagon were churning up.

Nothing, nothing at all was visible. Still the woman had the feeling that they were being watched, and a chill ran down her spine as she turned to gaze at the hills behind them. But again she could see nothing, not even an indication that there might be something. Her gaze moved ahead, past her husband and the lumbering oxen, past the small herd of livestock being hazed through the heavy growth along the creek by young Christian Kjerulf, and on up the sides of the hills. Quickly she moved her eyes, shifting her gaze from one point to another and back again, watching for anything that might have changed since her first view, and observing all possible cover.

The woman wasn't certain just what she was looking for, but she felt for some reason that the dust she had seen earlier had been raised by Indians. By now she had discarded the idea of soldiers, and there were relatively few outlaws or bad men in Utah Territory, at least in this area. One seldom if ever heard of a highway robbery. But they had been assured by Church leaders in Provo, prior to their move, that there would be no Indian problems, that the Utes under Arapene had been completely peaceful with the Mormons for more than a year, and that Black Hawk, Sanpitch, and others were not only friendly but openly anxious that the Mormons come settle in Sanpete Valley. They were, in fact, united with the Saints in opposition to Johnston's army, which was even then moving toward the valley.

For a moment the woman's gaze rested on a solitary circling buzzard, and she involuntarily shuddered as she watched that soaring symbol of death. Yet it was alone, and after a moment or so the woman knew that it was searching rather than waiting. Relieved that it was not acting as a prelude to disaster the woman again shifted her eyes.

How barren these hills appeared. How eternally barren. Could any land be more forsaken by all that was good and pleasing to the eye than this land was? Oh . . . what on earth was she doing here?

Most of the hills, especially to the north, were composed of yellow shale rock, with no vegetation except here and there a small clump of scrub oak, maple, manzanita, or a dwarf juniper or cedar tree as they were called locally.

Of course in the narrow valley along the creek there was a heavy growth of shrubbery, while thick green cheatgrass sloped upward toward the hills. But all this greenery did not fool the woman. She had seen cheatgrass before, and she knew that the green beauty would fade and die before the first of July and that then the grass would be useless to all but the hardiest of animals.

To the south on the steep slopes the oak and maple clumps were very thick, and jungle-like they rose sharply to finally join with the stately black pines towering so high above them. Even higher on the mountain she could see massive outcroppings of red stone, gigantic cliffs that she supposed would be called either Red Rocks or Red Cliffs.

Again the woman felt those uneasy stirrings along her neck, and almost instinctively she looked within the wagon, making certain of the baby girl's safety and yet conscious of the curious fact that she almost didn't care whether the child was safe or not.

How strange that she could feel that way. She knew it was wrong, she knew it was completely contrary to the doctrine of love for all people that Christ had taught and that her husband kept preaching, yet still she felt it. This little girl was not hers, and there was no way, no way at all, that she could love, or even be expected to love, as she would have loved her own. Nor for that matter would she allow herself to try. The pain caused by love, the price one had to pay for it, was just too high! Nothing was worth that price!

Another jolt in the wagon snapped the woman's neck, so she rose stiffly to her feet and climbed slowly to the ground. Perhaps if she walked she could get herself out of the somber mood she was in. Besides, it would lighten the load for the old oxen. Suddenly the incongruity of the situation struck the woman, and she almost laughed aloud thinking of it. Old oxen, old wagon, old men, young woman.

What a fine pioneer company they all made! If it wasn't so sad it could have been funny.

When the woman climbed out of the wagon Jens Terkelsen reined in his horse so he could more carefully observe her. Beyond a mild curiosity he had no particular interest in her as a person, and he was certain she felt an equal lack of interest in him. He watched her simply because he had organized this party, he owned the only horse in the group, and that made him responsible for those he traveled with, the woman included.

For the hundredth time, though, he found himself wondering about her. In the year he had known her she had spoken only rarely in his presence, and then usually to her husband. And so far he had never heard her name. That was the odd part. If her husband knew it he never spoke it, for Jens Terkelsen had never heard him call her anything but woman. The whole situation was strange, but with a shrug of his shoulders he put all thoughts of it aside. So long as she and the others did as he told them they could be as strange as they wanted to be. It surely didn't matter to him.

He thought then of their journey so far that day, mentally calculating how far they had come and the distance yet to go before they reached Uinta Springs, their camping place for the night. Of the four of them he alone had been through the canyon before, and he knew that on the other end of the barren canyon of Salt Creek stretched as fertile a valley as could be found in the whole territory, a valley just waiting for the plow, and a valley with a climate as near that of Denmark as any place he had seen since leaving there. Jens Terkelsen knew also that it was because of his insistence and leadership ability that the others were following him that day.

True it was that they had been instructed by the prophet, Brigham Young, to go on to Sanpete, but the others need never know that President Young had only called them because he, Jens Terkelsen, had suggested to him that he should. Yet even if Jens Jergensen knew that was why he had been called it would have made no difference. The call had still come from a prophet of God, so Jens Jergensen was bound to obey it and to fulfill it to the best of his ability. And therein, thought Brother Terkelsen, lay the success of Mormon colonization efforts. All went willingly, simply because they had to. God had spoken, and they could but obey. It was ridiculous, he thought, how gullible most people were. But not him, that was sure!

Jens Terkelsen, astride his big red stallion, had led the group out of Nephi while it was still dark, and by the time they reached the foothills the sky was beginning to gray behind the rising black hulk of Mount Nebo. The canyon at its mouth was narrow and choked with growth, and from this narrow mouth tumbled the churning and foaming waters of Salt Creek, a swiftly running stream that wandered down through the valley to finally lose itself in the thirsty earth off to the northwest. √

The heavy growth presented no real problems to Jens Terkelsen, mounted as he was, but it proved to be a real obstacle to the oxen and the single wagon they pulled. The oxen were old and tired easily, and they moved slowly, very slowly it seemed to him. Why, it seemed that every five minutes he was securing a rope to the wagon and helping to pull it out of some tight spot. If Brother Jergensen would just do a better job of driving he was certain they would have a great many fewer problems. But then, what could one expect?

Now where was that fool woman going? She surely ought to know better than to go climbing off in those hills. Jens Terkelsen was no frontiersman, but he had been in the West long enough to learn that people had to stick close together on the trail. Too many things could happen if one got separated from the others. He'd seen it happen. Especially when they were unarmed.

And that was something else that bothered him. In fact, it bothered him a lot. There wasn't a weapon in the whole party, and he felt uneasy because of it. True it was that he himself owned none. Fact is, he wouldn't have known what to do with a rifle or pistol had he owned one. But still he was surprised to learn that no one of the rest of the party owned a weapon either. Since Brother Jergensen was the only one with any tithing scrip, he had encouraged him to buy one at the Tithing Office, but the old blockhead had refused, saying that when men had weapons they were just naturally more inclined to fight. In Sanpete the Indians were at peace, and the only weapons he would need against them would be love and food. With those they could win over the hearts of all their Indian brothers. Besides, Brother Jergensen had continued, there were probably no weapons at the Tithing Office anyway, not with so many of the Mormon men armed and on military campaign, either out in Echo Canyon or exploring to the south for a new home for the Mormons. The previous fall he had given his own weapons to a brother who had been called to go with Lot Smith to slow down the government trains, and since that time he had felt no compulsion at all to obtain others. Leave firearms for those who needed them. He had the Gospel, and he had his testimony. Those were the only weapons he required.

Well, that was fine as far as it went, and he knew that Brigham Young taught that exact doctrine. But Jens Terkelsen also knew that Brother Brigham encouraged his Saints to be prepared for everything. In fact, when Brigham Young traveled around the Church his party was always armed, armed to the teeth and prepared for anything. This party, Jens Terkelsen knew, was not prepared to emigrate to Sanpete. At least they weren't ready as far as arms were concerned.

Of course Brother Terkelsen, while considering himself the captain of this small group, would never have admitted that he too was to blame for their lack of firearms. Not even to himself would he have admitted that, for though in reality he had quite a stack of Deseret Currency Association notes, and so was not a poor man himself, he gave no thought at all to procuring weapons for the group. The notes he held could be redeemed at Church headquarters for livestock from the Church herds, livestock meant wealth, and when he was finally settled he intended to be wealthy. That was his goal, pure and simple, and nothing would be allowed to interfere with it.

So he worried and did nothing else about it. And he did not worry without cause, though he himself knew nothing of the real reasons, nor likely ever would.

And the morning crawled slowly by, with sweat, curses, stubborn and tired animals, sticky biting flies, and choking dust the lot of the lonely travelers.

They nooned on a sandbar of Salt Creek, and while the woman got out flour and bacon young Christian gathered an armload of driftwood for the fire. With evident skill the woman selected the driest of the branches and quickly built a small fire, so small in fact that Jens Terkelsen marveled when the aroma of bacon and biscuits came to him. He would never have guessed that a fire so small could cook so much. He noted too that there was virtually no smoke, and so as he relaxed in the shade of a cottonwood he wondered again about the woman. In spite of himself he was impressed. She was young, but somewhere, sometime, this woman had been up the river and over the pass, as young Christian would put it.

The baby had been fussing for some time before the woman was really aware of it, so far away had been her thoughts, but now she went slowly to the wagon and removed the infant from her box. In spite of herself she thought of how beautiful this little girl was. Three months old and already she was so alert. Miserably she wondered how it was possible for her to love and detest this little tyke so much all at the same time. Oh, why did everything have to be so confused and so complicated?

The crying stopped once the woman had changed the soiled diaper, and soon the baby too was getting her noontime meal, gurgling and cooing in between her slurping suckling.

She glanced over at Jens and surprised him looking at her with a look of such love and devotion that she had to turn quickly away to keep from crying.

Ah, what an unfair life this was! Three months ago Jens had been ready to welcome into the world his first two children, his "Blessed Posterity" as he called them. For with a strange twist of fate his wife of twenty years and his wife of ten months were due to deliver their very first children within weeks of each other.

Kjersta had gone into labor first, but with complications and her years against her she had passed away within minutes of childbirth. The blow to old Jens had been terrible, so the woman had cared for the now motherless infant through the night while Jens sat near the bed of his departed wife.

The next day she herself had gone into premature labor, probably caused by the emotional shock of the day before, and that night her own little son had been born. He was so tiny, so cute, so special, and he lived, despite her desperate pleas to heaven, for just three hours before he too was gone.

Oh the grief, the agony! How could she carry on? How could she nurse another woman's child when her own lay dead on the pillow beside her? It was not fair, it was not right!

It had been the hardest thing she had ever done, taking care of that child for the next three months, but she had done it because it had to be done. There was no choice. Yet every moment she expected that it too would die, die as all the others had, leaving her alone once more. And it would die, that she knew. It was only a question of when, that was all. A question of when, and also a question of if. *If* she would be there, and she wouldn't be. Not anymore, not anymore forever. Somehow she was going to get out of that suffering, she was going to walk away, she . . .

Further thought was interrupted by that familiar tingling sensation on the back of her neck. There! On the ridge to the east was a haze of dust again. Dust raised by an unseen rider, dust raised by someone who was following them. The woman was certain of it.

They were being followed!

CHAPTER THREE

"Hei, Christian! Come und halp me, vill you? Dis vone ox she no dang good! She don't know a thing und ve be stuck again! I say, vill you come und halp me?"

Christian Kjerulf groaned aloud and turned back toward the wagon. For a moment he stood still, wiping the sweat from his grimy face with the sleeve of his shirt. Jumping blue blazes, how his eyes burned! They felt like fisheyes stuck into a sandbank and then put back again. Why, this must be the hundredth time he had gone back to pull that doggone wagon out of some hole or other, and what with that and chasing those fool cows and calves all over the canyon he was about as limp as a neck-wrung rooster and as sweaty as a hog butcher in frost time. Scrud! He'd more'n likely walked the entire thirteen miles to Uinta Springs three times already that day, and they weren't yet halfway there.

And what, he asked himself aloud, about that beanpole Terkelsen up there on the hill sitting astride his fancy horse? How come that skinny so-and-so didn't herd the doggone cattle instead of prancing his horse along up there on that fool mountain?

Guarding them! You bet your best homespun britches he was! And from what? Mountain lions? Ha ha! It sure as blue blazes wasn't Indians. Old Terkelsen wouldn't know an Indian if he saw one. Which he sure wasn't likely to. Even if he did, how was he going to do anything about it? He didn't have a gun, and even if he'd had one Christian figured he'd be such a lousy shot he couldn't hit the ground one round out of three. Why, he was so doggone cautious about his own hide that he'd ride a mile just to spit. Shoot, if old Terkelsen ever ran into Indians he'd have about as much chance as a one-legged man in a kicking contest, and that would help the rest of them about as much as sitting down on a rattlesnake with a toothache. Anyway a man would think that with a horse like that Terkelsen would enjoy hazing those cattle through the brush. It was a cutting horse anyhow, and it sure as blue blazes would make the job easier.

Cows surely were crazy critters. For a while they would go along nice and easy as could be, then a chipmunk or something would spook them and off they'd go in forty different directions, making themselves about as scarce as bird dung in a cuckoo clock. Then, after about an hour of rounding them all back up, they wouldn't be driven for sour apples the whole rest of the day.

And now old Jergensen needed help back at the wagon. Again! Well, he'd help, but phooey with those dang cows. Let Terkelsen round them up. Him and his dang fancy horse.

"My boy, ve have got troubles here. Very big troubles. Ja?"

"Yeh, I guess you do. How come you went and got it stuck again? Can't you see it wouldn't go through here?"

"First, my boy, do not speak to your elders like that. Second, it vas not my fault. Dis vone ox she don't know vich vay is gee und vich vay is haw, und now the vheels are stuck und ve don't go anyvhere. Vat you tink ve do now?"

Quickly Christian Kjerulf surveyed the situation. One thing was certain. They sure as blue blazes were stuck. The big rear wheels were jammed between two boulders, and it was going to take more than just a little pushing to get them out. It looked to him as though they were going to have to unhitch the team, secure them to the rear of the wagon, and pull it out backward.

He said as much to Jens Jergensen, putting into his voice just enough of an air of nonchalance to hide the pride he felt in being the one-and-only that was relied upon to get them out of trouble. Scrud! He ought to be the captain of the company, instead of old Terkelsen.

Dumb oxen, hah! Christian knew how Jens Jergensen had gotten them stuck. He geed when he ought to be hawing, and he was for-ever using the trace chain to keep his balance, pulling the oxen out of line every time he did so. And he did it no matter how many times he had it pointed out to him the trouble it caused. Scrud! Sometimes Christian even wondered if the old man had sense enough to spit downwind.

Yet Christian knew that Jens Jergensen was a good man. He had been his father's friend back in the old country. In fact, that was why Christian was with him now. Jens Jergensen and his wife had joined the Mormon Church the same day he and his father had joined. When it came time to emigrate to America he had accompanied

Brother and Sister Jergensen instead of his father, who had suddenly become too ill to travel. For nearly three years they had been with the Saints in Utah, and for most of that time the old couple had been the only parents Christian had. He had received word of his own father's death shortly after his arrival in Utah Territory, and the Jergensens had cared for him since then.

Well, they had cared for him mostly. Right after entering the valley he'd gone to work with the Church public works program, hauling timber, working on the fort and the temple, building roads and bridges and so on. So it could never be said that anyone had cared for him totally. By jumping blue blazes, he could take care of himself, and this forced move to the south was only serving to prove it. Yessirree, by thunder, he was a man now, an American man! Maybe in Sanpete he'd have the chance to show that to everyone.

Christian Kjerulf glanced up to see if Jens Terkelsen was coming to help, and when he saw that he wasn't he bent to the task of uncoupling the yoke of oxen himself.

Terkelsen! He had been with them ever since they had left Denmark too, and he was so unlike the solid Jergensen that Christian couldn't understand why they were so close to one another.

Old Terkelsen was skinnier than a wet weasel and so tall he had to shorten his stirrups to keep his feet from dragging. He smiled so rarely you'd have thought he'd been weaned on a pickle, and Christian would have bet a double eagle he had calluses from patting himself on the back. Yet somehow he and Jergensen were close enough that it wouldn't have surprised him to see them sharing the same toothpick.

Terkelsen had never married, showed no real desire to, and seemed only to tolerate Kjersta, Jergensen's first wife. Christian would never forget how shocked Terkelsen had been when Jens and Kjersta had announced that Jens was about to take him a plural wife.

Neither he nor Terkelsen had known the woman, but jumping blue blazes how he'd argued with Brother Jergensen about it. He'd got so excited he was bouncing up and down like a barrel rolling downhill, throwing out arguments to beat the band, yelling such things as he didn't know her, he was too old to go into polygamy, she was too young to marry an old geezer like him, Kjersta would get jealous, and on and on. Old Jergensen had merely smiled at him and waited until he ran out of things to say. When at last that unlikely event occurred he softly explained that he felt from prayer and inspiration that he was to marry her, that she would make a good wife, and that she would help him and Kjersta to one day have a family.

Oh how the two of them had laughed at him then. Christian felt ashamed just thinking about it. Brother Jergensen had stood for a moment gaping at them with a look of disbelief which changed quickly to one of such hurt and pain that Christian knew he would never forget it for the rest of his life. Then with tears in his eyes he simply took the arm of his wife, turned, and walked out.

When he came back a few days later to their cabin south of Little Cottonwood the woman was with him, looking younger and prettier than Christian had ever guessed she would. That had been over a year ago, and now here they were in Salt Creek Canyon going to what they hoped would be a new home with a sure-enough family.

Old Jens actually had a child. Two of them, in fact! When Christian had learned that both wives were expecting, he'd been just as surprised as the little porcupine who awoke to find he'd spent the night cuddled up to a cactus. And the young man must have said something, too. For Brother Jergensen, bless his ever-trying heart, had immediately reached for his scriptures and read to Christian the account of Sarah giving Abraham Hagar her handmaid to wife, and of how eventually both women, old and young, had conceived and borne Abraham children.

That made it, to Brother Jergensen, a purely common event, nothing to be wondered at. He somehow just didn't understand that he wasn't like old Abraham at all. He wasn't a prophet, so he couldn't compare himself like that. But Brother Jergensen quickly climbed over that little obstacle by telling him that it didn't matter. What counted was the faith you had, prophet or no. And that was that! Why, for proof of what he said, there were his two wives growing big with child. And Christian had to admit that it was pretty hard to argue with facts like those.

Since then a lot of things had changed. Brother Jergensen had lost one wife and one child, but he was not at all bitter, claiming instead that he felt he should rejoice because God was anxious to take two of his family home to Him where they could be eternally happy. Besides, he was quick to point out that he still had a lovely wife and a beautiful little daughter with him, and how could he be more blessed than that? Again, how could Christian argue? He did have a baby, and he was scared to death of the little thing. Christian had never seen him hold her, though he did like to poke her and make funny little noises at her. He sounded silly as blue blazes, but strangely enough the little girl seemed to like it.

Once the oxen were uncoupled he led them to the rear of the wagon to secure them there, only half listening to the heavily accented comments of Jens Jergensen, knowing that he was speaking more to himself than to anyone else.

One of Christian Kjerulf's greatest accomplishments, he felt, was being able to speak as the native Americans did. In three years of working on the public works program he had totally eliminated his own accent, and he was, as he liked to say, proud as blue blazes of it. He'd been told he had more verbal lather than a shaving mug, and he considered that a fine compliment. This country held great potential for him, and he was thrilled that he was going to help open up Sanpete Valley to settlement. Christian had great confidence in the leaders of the Church and was certain they were inspired. But he had at least equal confidence in himself. Why, the situation in Sanpete was perfect for one such as he, alone and with no family responsibilities. He would receive a stewardship from the bishop of at least twenty or thirty acres plus a town lot. He could work hard, and in no time at all he would be a major landholder in Sanpete, a power to be reckoned with. The only flaw he could see in his plan was that the U. S. Government might not honor Mormon land distribution. Either that or drive them all into the wilderness again with that stupid mob called an army that Buchanan had sent to kill all the Mormons. The army that they were even then, in a sense, fleeing from. But either way, losing land or losing homes, everyone else would be floating along in the same boat he was sailing. So why worry! Yes indeed! The future did look bright to Christian E. Kjerulf.

The woman, tiring of the wait while the wagon was being pulled out, walked away toward the east scouting for sign. Skirting a small ravine she was careful to watch for rattlesnakes, of which she had a terrible fear, but as she brushed through the fragrant sage and rabbit brush all thoughts of snakes and other worries left her and she found herself becoming enthralled with the barren beauty of the country. In its unique way, she thought, it might even be considered attractive.

The mountains seemed to go on forever, and each more distant range carried its own distinctive hue of blue and purple. The vegetation, though scant, had a remarkable degree of variation. Even the spiny prickly-pear cactus had beautiful flowers. There was wildlife too, for early that morning she had seen three deer. They were a doe and two fawns, and they had only moved away when she got within a few yards of them.

The fragrant beauty of the hills had a soothing effect upon the woman, and as she slowly walked along she found that a feeling of peace and calmness was relieving her mind.

Deep within her heart she knew it was wrong to feel as she did about Jens and his daughter, or to question the Church and its doctrine of polygamy. It was funny, but it had not been very long since she had known with total assurity that the Church was true, that it contained the fullness of the Gospel of Jesus Christ, and that polygamy was a part of that truth. But now she found herself doubting, really questioning for the first time in all her life. Jens had told her over and over that God tested people by giving them trials, and if that was true, and if there was a God, then she was surely being tested. She really should want to raise that little girl, to show her the marvelous beauty of the world, to teach her of fine things and how to appreciate them, and especially the little child should learn to have love for others, though heaven knew how she would ever teach that when she was having such a struggle with love herself.

And Jens, she had to admit that in his own funny way he was a good man. Certainly he was an idealist, so deeply devoted to his religion and to his God that she thought of it as fanaticism. Yet he had never physically abused her and he certainly tried to be kind to her. If only he wasn't so . . . so opposite to what she felt represented true manhood. He seemed to her a weakling, fumbling and bumbling his way through life, led here and there at the will of Jens Terkelsen, that arrogant old man who was forever prancing around foolishly on the back of that ridiculously beautiful stallion. Brother Terkelsen was crazy bringing such an animal out into this wilderness. Any Indian alive would give his right arm for an animal like that, and so, for that matter, would a lot of white men.

How her father would have loved that horse, and what marvelous things a man like him might have done with an animal like that. But he could never have afforded such an animal. He was always too busy moving to greener pastures, only none of them ever turned out to be as green as he had expected.

Absolutely nothing in her life ever seemed to work out fairly. Never! Sometimes she found herself wishing she was dead, only she didn't really because she was so afraid of it. Jens said that death held no terrors for him, for he knew what awaited him on the other side. Perhaps he did, but she could claim no such peace of mind. Death to her seemed an awful blackness, a bitter void, a total ending that mocked all one did or tried to do and achieve in this life. Death made the whole of existence pointless, and only misery remained as the final outcome of all endeavors.

She thought again of her husband. He was so proud of his baby daughter, and daily he thanked his God that in his old age he had been blessed with posterity. That, he told the woman, was one of the reasons why he had no fear of death. How could a man be totally gone when some of him remained behind in the form of his posterity?

Posterity!

He placed such importance on posterity. Why couldn't he see, after all he had been through, how quickly death could and would destroy a man's children. Then he would be left with nothing, nothing but the bitter mockery of his dreams, dashed to pieces on the jagged rocks of death.

Well, maybe Jens couldn't see it, but the woman could. Oh how she could! And she was certain that one day he too would know, and then let him talk about his faith.

Pausing to catch her breath the woman realized that she had come farther than she had intended and climbed much higher than it was safe to do. Glancing back she could see the wagon and the three men working on it, and they looked so small from this distance, like ants scurrying about. If she stayed under that old juniper across the draw before her until the wagon was freed she could probably intercept it directly down from where she stood. It shouldn't take them too much longer to free the wagon and get on their way again, and the baby should sleep for at least another hour, so why not rest. It would surely feel good just lying in the shade for a spell.

Accordingly the woman turned and started moving down the slope into the grassy draw where the juniper stood, for once not paying a great deal of attention to the hills around her. She was almost there when she heard the rattle of stones ahead of her and up the hill on the other side of the draw.

Instinctively she looked up, and to her horror she saw, not seventy yards away, what looked like an Indian pony partially hidden in a clump of oak, pawing its front hoof impatiently as it waited. Had it not been for the small noise it made with its hoof she would never have seen it, but now that she had, what was she to do?

The wagon was out of sight beyond the ridge she had just descended, and she knew the men were too far away to be of any help if she cried out. Besides, maybe the Indian or Indians had not yet seen her. If she screamed that would surely attract their attention.

No, the best and very likely only thing to do was to continue walking down the draw, acting nonchalant but in reality going as rapidly as she could without appearing to be in a hurry. That way she might make it.

Instantly then she started, and though she thoroughly examined the terrain as she walked she could discover no Indians. Of course that meant little and she knew it, for Indians were seen when they wanted to be seen, and not much more often.

She was in the bottom now, moving as steadily as she dared toward the mouth of the draw, and as she walked she thought about her long skirts and how they were hiding to some extent her scurrying feet. Wasn't it ridiculous the silly things a person could think of at a time like this? It was almost like that . . .

There, up on the hill! Behind her a little, near where the horse was hidden, an Indian had risen to a crouching position. It was too far away to distinguish features, but she could almost see him hesitate, trying to decide whether to run after her or to use his horse.

How had he hidden there? Where he stood there was no cover, no cover at all, and the woman knew she had looked directly at that spot at least a half-dozen times and yet had seen nothing.

Not looking directly at him she kept up her steady pace, fighting down a terrible urge to run, not wanting to commit herself until the Indian did, not wanting him to know that she had seen him.

For an instant only the Ute hesitated, and then throwing caution to the wind he bounded down the hill in pursuit of the woman, his disfigured face almost glowing with a savage lust.

Within seconds the woman too was in full flight, her skirts held high as she raced desperately for the mouth of the draw. Oh if she could only get to where the men in the wagon could see and hear her. She so desperately wanted to cry out, to scream, but somehow from within her came the knowledge that she would need all her wind for running.

The woman ran without looking back, knowing as she ran almost where the Ute was by the occasional rattle of gravel or the swishing of brush as he leaped through it.

He was close, much closer than she had guessed he could be in such a short time. O dear God, she prayed, help me . . . please . . .

Why was he so silent? Why didn't he yell and scream as Indians usually did? Why . . .

Run! Move your legs faster . . . faster . . . Don't trip . . . watch where you're going . . . but hurry! Above all else, hurry! He's right behind you! Run . . . !

Instinctively now she found herself hunching her shoulders as she fled from the mouth of the draw, expecting at any instant the agonizing thrust of an arrow, knife, or bullet into her spine. But no, as she tore around the rocky point into full view of the wagon and heard at last the muffled shouts of Christian and her husband she was still uninjured and still at least ten yards ahead of the desperately running Indian.

At last the woman's terror overcame her reason and she fled headlong across the flat, screaming as she ran. She was yelling nothing coherent, yet her voice carried with it the feeling of urgency she so desperately needed to convey.

Jens Jergensen, his squat but powerful body straining against the wagon box, was the first to hear the screams of his wife. Jens, though he never spoke of it, prided himself a little on his great physical strength. Usually, when he took hold on something and put his mind to it, that object went about where he wanted it to go. And so as he heard the screaming of his wife he gave a mighty heave on the wagon and with a great screech it lunged free, dropping Jens Jergensen to the earth in a heap.

Jens Terkelsen and Christian Kjerulf heard her screams also, but Terkelsen's horse suddenly twisted so that the man was entangled in the rope he was using to help free the wagon.

Christian, on the other hand, came lunging up out of the wash to see what was wrong, stumbled over the wagon tongue, and sprawled head on into Jens Jergensen, who was just then getting to his own feet. They both sprawled back to earth.

So it was that none of them saw the single Ute warrior slide to a halt, observe the fleeing woman and the wagon for just an instant, and then wheel and race silently back into the draw from which he and the woman had so recently erupted.

None of them saw anything, she alone excepted. It was precious little for five lives to hang by.

CHAPTER FOUR

Hoskoots, the Ugly one, was puzzled. Total silence reigned around him, and things were not as he expected them to be. In all the experience gained in one short life there was nothing which he could draw upon to explain the events of this day. Thus he was spending long minutes considering.

He lay in the open on a barren hillside with no cover save a small clump of grass near his shoulders. Yet his dark body blended so well with his surroundings that very few would ever have seen him there.

Hoskoots knew this, just as he knew that one usually looked for enemies in places where they might be concealed. The Ute, a clever man, had quickly learned that a man usually saw about what he expected to see. Few would ever expect to see a warrior lying on an open hillside in broad light of day with no cover at all. Therefore Hoskoots had the best cover of all, the cover found in his enemy's mind. And Hoskoots did have enemies.

So he waited. All was quiet, all was still. Only the wind stirred the long grass on the slope. Downhill a lizard scurried from the shade of one clump of fragrant sage to another, pausing along the way to stare with heaving sides at the still form of the Ute. Uphill a jay sat in a juniper and scolded angrily, and for a moment it sounded to Hoskoots as though the jay was disturbed by something. Yet there was nothing there and so he dismissed it from his mind and continued to wait through the silence of the afternoon.

Most white men have noted Indians for their curiosity, and though they more than likely were no more curious than any other people, Hoskoots definitely was a curious man. Whatever did not fit in with his own understanding of things as they should have been was worth considering, and Hoskoots was a great considerer. He had learned early that after due consideration all things could be understood, so the Ute warrior prided himself on his great understanding of his world.

It had been his curiosity, this desire to fit all things into place in his mind, that had led him to this barren hillside in the beginning. That and the squawpulling, of course.

It started with the bawling calves. True there was nothing unusual about bawling calves, at least there was nothing unusual if they were bawling where calves ought to be bawling. But these weren't and that meant either they were strays and would be worth securing or they were with a party of whites, Mormonees or Mericats, and said party could mean the wealth he so desperately needed to purchase Chipetz. Either way the thing was worth investigation and Hoskoots did not hesitate to do so.

From behind an outcropping of sandstone on the rim of the narrow canyon of Salt Creek Hoskoots first observed the single wagon and its four occupants. His alert eye missed nothing. He quickly noted the young man herding the stock, the heavy man walking near the two oxen which drew the wagon forward, the woman on the wagon seat, and the thin man on the red horse. He saw no arms in evidence and concluded that their weapons must be in the wagon.

He was unable to tell if these whites were Mormonees, the followers of the Great Mormonee Brigham Young, or Mericats, those other whites who came from far away. No, he wasn't certain, but his guess was that they were Mormonees. It made no difference, though, no difference at all. Not since Hoskoots had first set his eyes upon the red stallion.

Carefully he studied it. The stallion was a beautiful animal, fully sixteen hands, and the Ute had never seen a horse move so smoothly. He was transfixed by the beauty of the muscles rippling beneath the skin, and the sheen of its coat in the morning light was something to behold. Never had an animal moved the Indian as this one did. The stallion must be his. No, the stallion *would* be his! There was no doubt now, no doubt at all. In just hours the lovely Chipetz would be his.

Hoskoots had to have that horse. Try as he would, though, he could think of no way to secure it without great personal risk. For a warrior Hoskoots was famous even among his own people for the care he took of his own skin. Hoskoots was no gambler, at least not with his own life. He never moved until he was certain that all the consequences would be advantageous to himself. Likewise he never engaged in battle unless he was certain that he had an edge. In this he was scorned by some of the People, but Hoskoots cared little for their scorn. Instead he rode alone and mostly enjoyed it. And he remained with a reasonably whole skin.

That was why he was so puzzled about the events of the past hour. Oo-ah! What a blunder! In spite of his usual caution he had about thrown all away not long before, and according to his reasoning he should either be dead by nor or else involved in his great final battle.

Yet here he was on the hill. The long grass continued to whisper in the wind and nothing else moved. Anywhere.

Perhaps he had missed something, something that even now, if considered properly, might save his life. Carefully, in the heat of the afternoon sun, Hoskoots went over in his mind again and again the events of the day. So engrossed was he in his considerations that he failed to notice the jay's sudden departure from the old juniper uphill from him. If he had he might also have seen the still brown from of Inepegut, the Crazy Man, a burning light in his eyes, fingering absently the thong of his bow. He might have noticed these things, and he should have, for by such small things is the destiny of man shaped.

Throughout the morning and early afternoon he had ridden roughly parallel to the canyon and so the course of the wagon. Frequently he paused to make a cautious approach to the rim of the canyon. He told himself that he did this to observe the progress of the wagon, but he knew better. He could hear the wagon well enough to know where it was. It was simply that he couldn't resist watching his stallion, for already he considered the beautiful animal as his own personal property.

A horse was probably the most important single piece of property that a Ute brave could own. A rifle was important too, as was a wife and perhaps two wives, though many men got along well without either rifles or wives. But one was not a man without a horse. And a great horse, or a whole string of them? Hoskoots could hardly imagine the honor and prestige that a man might have, the honor and prestige that he had never had. Why, with that horse he might even be able to own several maidens.

That, too, was important, for Hoskoots wanted very badly to own Chipetz, and perhaps other squaws also. Until now he had always been alone, unable to get any of the maidens to do more than just laugh at him. Of course he knew it was his face they were laughing at, for wasn't he named Hoskoots, the Ugly One?

He agonized over his face, and considered it a punishment for something, though what that was he could not imagine. After all, it had not been really his fault when the wild pony had rearranged things on the front of his head with a well-placed hind hoof. For a little he thought he was dead, and then for days wished he was, but the whole thing slowly knit together and healed. True, there were some great changes from what his mother had originally done with him prior to his birth, yet inside he was still the same with all the same wants and needs as any Ute warrior. He wanted a squaw. And now he would have one.

For now he would have the red horse.

When those of the wagon halted for their noon rest Hoskoots halted too, and from a place of concealment he carefully observed their actions. Perhaps now would come his opportunity.

Hoskoots was greatly interested in the activities of the woman as she prepared the meal, and as he watched her a plan began to form in his mind.

The old man seemed always to ride the horse, and all morning he had ridden up the hill and slightly ahead of the wagon. And he carried no weapon. Here and for some distance ahead the brush was thick and heavy on the south of the canyon so it was likely that the horse would continue to be ridden on Hoskoot's side. If all this continued to be so, and he saw no reason that it wouldn't, then the Ute had but to position himself in some draw out of sight of the wagon, wait for the old man on the horse to reach him, ambush the man, and ride off on his red stallion. The plan was perfect. If done correctly, no one, including the old man, would ever know what had happened and Hoskoots would be safely away on his stallion.

The Ugly One considered the plan carefully, and the more he thought of it the more he liked it. There was no personal risk in it at all.

Scouting ahead of the wagon party he found exactly the spot where an ambush would work. It was a steep little draw that cut diagonally down into the valley of Salt Creek. When the old man rode his horse into that draw he would be out of sight of the wagon just long enough for Hoskoots to kill him and get the horse.

Hiding his own pony carefully the Ute positioned himself and began to wait.

If he thought of it at all the Ute spent little time worrying that the whites were Mormonees, the Ute name for the members of the Church of Jesus Christ of Latter-day Saints. Nor did he consider the fact that Wakera, before his death, had been great friends with Brigham Young and that even then, June 1858, Arapene, their current head chief, had worked out an agreement with Brigham Young where both the People and the Mormonees would fight together to drive off the Mericat army that was coming in to fill up their valleys. He failed even to recall that the Mormonees were coming into Sanpete at the request of Sanpitch, the chief of his own band. After all, what was all that compared to the value and beauty of the red stallion?

The Utes generally were considered a superstitious people. Much of a warrior's life was directed by what he felt from the influence of spirits. All Utes were very much afraid of witches and crazy or insane people no matter what their race, and they believed that one whose name was placed on paper would die.

So Hoskoots prepared to kill for his horse. He was convinced that the spirits had given him that stallion as a reward for his valor, for hadn't he been led directly to it? Just what act of valor he was being rewarded for the Ute wasn't sure of either, but still, that must be why he had been led to the horse. The spirits obviously wanted him to have Chipetz.

Most Indians were noted also for their great patience, but in this virtue Hoskoots was somewhat deficient. He was aware of this flaw in his character but spent little time worrying about it. To correct it would have taken time and effort, and he just didn't have the patience to do that.

For more than an hour Hoskoots had lain silently on the hillside, but things were taking too long and he was worried. The old man on the horse should have been there by now. There could be no good reason for a delay such as this.

He was so engrossed in his worry about his horse that the woman was almost in the bottom of the draw before he even saw her, and then he was so surprised that for a moment he failed to do anything about it, thus losing a few very precious seconds.

Suddenly though it dawned on him what possibilities he might have if he captured her, and with that thought he lunged to his feet. His pony was close, but he knew he could easily outrun the woman on foot, so down the hill he sped, his eyes never leaving the woman.

Like most humans Hoskoots was an opportunist, and in an instant the horse and all else was forgotten. There was nothing in his life now but the woman, and her capture had become in an instant his only goal.

Only the woman was closer to the mouth of the draw than he at first anticipated, and she was also running faster than she appeared to be. He was still a full ten yards behind her, intently, silently, following, when he gasped in horror and realized that he had run into full view of the wagon and the Mormonees.

Instantly all thoughts of the woman and the red stallion fled from his mind. In a panic he slid to a stop, whirled, and sped back up the draw to his horse, fearing at any moment the sharp reports of the Mormonee rifles.

Hoskoots had a good pony, one that could run all day, but he had seen that red stallion and knew that it could run circles around his own horse. So Hoskoots the Ugly One prepared for death, and while he prepared he watched for another ambush site. Though he were to die he would do so as a man of the People. And he would not take that final journey alone.

That was when he saw the hill and beyond it the copse of aspen where he might hide his pony. In minutes there was no sign of his presence, and to the casual observer he might have appeared as just another rock on the hillside.

Nevertheless, he was observed, but not by a casual observer. The one who watched was even more proficient in the fine art of concealment than the wily Hoskoots. For Hoskoots was watched by Inepegut, the Crazy Man, the Killer of his own kind, the most feared of all the Utes.

More time passed and still Hoskoots waited, but the puzzlement was growing. There was no dust to indicate that riders followed him, no sound on the hill except the occasional whir of insects. Where were the Mormonees?

For long moments Hoskoots lay still and considered his problem. All was still in the afternoon sun, and only occasionally did a wandering breeze shift the long grass or fluff the aspen leaves into dancing where his pony waited. Still the Ugly One lay quietly and considered.

It must be so, he thought suddenly. Yes, it must be so! The only reason the whites were not after him, the only reason that he could accept as rational, was that they had not seen him. True, the woman had been running, but as he thought back it was in his memory that she was running even before he started after her. That would mean that she was running for some reason other than fear of himself. She was running from something or toward something that had nothing at all to do with him.

That made sense to the Ute, much sense. Especially when he recalled that he had neither heard nor seen any activity around the wagon during the brief time when he had been visible to its occupants.

Suddenly Hoskoots grinned. They had not seen him! None of the whites had seen him at all. He had been so silent that the woman was not aware of him, and he had been so swift that none of the men near the wagon had seen him either. That was why there was no pursuit. That was why he was still alone upon the hillside. If they had seen him they would most certainly have given chase. They hadn't, and so his chances of obtaining the red stallion were as good as ever. It was obvious that the spirits were still smiling upon him.

Still grinning, Hoskoots rose to his feet and ran to where his pony was hidden. Mounting, he turned its head back toward Salt Creek Canyon, his mind already considering new plans for obtaining his horse.

And so the Ugly One rode toward a beautiful red stallion. Yet he also rode toward much more than that. Then too, he did not exactly ride alone. Not if the shadow called Inepegut, drifting along silently behind him, counted at all.

CHAPTER FIVE

With a powerful heave Jens Jergensen threw the wildly struggling body of Christian Kjerulf to the side, and lunging to his feet he sprinted toward his screaming wife. His eyes scanned the serrated ridges and barren hills beyond her as he ran, but he could see nothing that might cause her alarm, nothing at all.

He could not imagine that it was Indians, for they were supposed to be at peace with the Utes. Yet he could think of nothing else that might cause his wife to behave in this way. Whatever it was, it must have been bad, for he had never seen her act like this. Not ever!

"O God in heaven," he cried as he ran, "please let my voman be all right . . . Halp me to take care of her, halp me, I pray . . ."

At last he reached her and the woman stumbled sobbing into his arms. Desperately she looked into his face, trying to warn him, trying to tell him of the danger. But the terror had been too great and she fainted, slumping against his powerful old body.

Jens Jergensen quickly laid his beloved young wife upon the ground and hastily examined her. Nowhere could he find anything wrong. Her heartbeat was slowing to near normal, and as her breathing became less ragged he decided that the screams had been caused by fright rather than injury.

Standing then the powerful old man easily lifted the woman in his arms and walked slowly back to the wagon, his eyes never leaving the unconscious face of his wife.

It was not many moments before she opened her eyes, and she did so to find herself lying on a blanket in the shade of the wagon. Her husband had moistened a rag in the creek and was wiping her forehead while the other two men crowded in close trying to ease their own helplessness.

The woman struggled to rise, unable to understand why they were not moving, why they were not attempting to hook up the oxen.

"Jens," she pleaded as he attempted to push her back onto the blanket. "Jens, let me up! We have to get out of here! We've got to leave . . ."

"Hush, voman. You are all right. There is no need for fear. There is no need . . ."

"Christian," the woman shouted. "Get the oxen hooked up. We must go back. We . . ."

"Go back? Vat ve vant to go back for?"

"Indians, Brother Terkelsen. There are Indians here, and we are in danger. I know!"

"Bah," snorted the stubborn Terkelsen. "There can be no Indians here. Ve have seen no sign of them."

"You may not have, but I did."

"Ja, sure you did. Sure you did. Vat vould they vant here? Vat vould they vant vith us? Don't you know that Brother Brigham said ve vere at peace vith them?"

Jens Jergensen, quiet up to now, gently broke into the heated conversation.

"Voman, are you certain? Vere did you see them?"

In anguish the woman turned her head and nodded toward the draw. This was taking far too much time! Why couldn't they just believe her?

"Of course I saw only one," she cried, "but there were probably more. You don't often see Indians, not unless they want you to. But I don't have to see them to know they are around."

"Ah, how do you know?" queried Christian. "If you can't see something, then how in blue blazes do you know it's there?"

Slowly the woman turned to face him.

"By their habits, Christian. I saw one brave, and where there is one there are usually others. If you want more, then I will tell you that we have been followed most of the day by at least one of them, for several times I have seen his dust."

At this last statement the men started in disbelief, and young Christian almost broke out laughing. Dust? What next, he wondered.

"Besides," she continued, and she added this carefully, almost knowing beforehand what their reaction would be, "I have been feeling them, feeling someone watching us off and on all day."

For a moment there was absolute silence, and then Jens Terkelsen bellowed out.

"Feeling them! Feeling them! I vant to know how vone feels an Indian?"

The woman, becoming more frustrated by the moment, tried in vain to tell them about the eerie feeling along her spine, but at this Christian and Jens Terkelsen broke into laughter and her husband rose to his feet in confused silence, glancing back and forth from his friends to his wife.

"Christian! Brother Terkelsen! Why won't you listen? What must I do to prove to you that I am right? I say I have feelings about the Indians and you laugh. Then you say you know the Church is true because you have feelings and you weep for joy and say God has given you a testimony. Where is there a difference? Feelings are still feelings. Always have been, always will be. And mine are every bit as important as yours. Besides, remember that I have seen the Indian and the dust."

"I don't know about that," muttered Christian, "but I do know your feelings ain't the same thing as ours. Ours is religious."

"Now, Christian," Jens finally said, "I think you be wrong in that. Vat you think the Lord vas speaking of ven He said He vould bless us in all our doings? Vat is the sense of praying over our homes, our flocks, our fields, und so on if all He vill help us in is religion? Ja, you see that vould make a pretty dumb religion, und God vould be a pretty limited God. Ja, you must believe as you vill, but as for me, I can't believe in any such narrow-minded Being. My Heavenly Father has promised that He vill vatch over me und mine in all things, und by golly I believe Him!"

For a moment the three sat silent, and only Jens Jergensen didn't turn his face from the woman's accusing eyes.

Suddenly he turned toward the draw.

"Ja," he shouted, "ve settle this now. I believe my voman, but no matter. Ve vill all go now to see the canyon, und then ve vill know. Voman, you stay here und rest. Ve be back shortly."

Jens Jergensen took the pitchfork from the wagon and stalked off toward the mouth of the draw, while Jens Terkelsen, tall, thin, old, and hard as nails, and Christian E. Kjerulf, young, strong, and full of plans, followed behind. And as they walked they grinned and made funny little comments, and they failed to see the black look that darkened Jens Jergensen's face as he listened to them.

Angrily and almost helplessly he looked at the pitchfork gripped tightly in his hand, and once again he thought of his decision not to bring weapons along. Of course that wasn't really true, for he sincerely doubted that he could have found weapons for sale even if he had tried. The army marching toward the territory was too much of a threat, and those who had weapons wanted to keep them. Still, if they had been available would he have brought them? Probably, but not with the intent of using them. His past life had taught him that it was too easy to use them for the wrong reasons, and that life had ended when he was baptized. A gun might be used for obtaining food, but never to fight with. If it ever came to fighting, and he was forced into it, then he could do so without guns. But before that event he would do all in his power to maintain peace. To remain true to himself it was all he could do.

For thirty minutes they scoured the canyon, but untrained as they were they could see nothing out of the ordinary. Tiny grasshoppers fled before the men as they returned, arguing and speculating as they went. And as they walked, Hoskoots the Ugly One lay on a barren hillside not more than three miles away. He hid with no cover to hide him, and already he was growing impatient waiting for the impending attack.

On reaching the wagon the men were startled to find the yoke of oxen hooked to the trace chains, the tongue in place, and the wagon ready to roll.

The woman was sitting on a stone under a nearby cottonwood patiently nursing the gurgling little baby, and as the man called Jens Jergensen searched her face he found nothing to indicate her thoughts. Her face was closed. She merely waited and said nothing.

Jens Terkelsen averted his eyes as he walked past the woman. Though he did it as an overt act of modesty the woman knew there was more to it than that.

This man, stubborn as he was, would not admit that there were Indians or that there was danger from them, even if he thought there was. The woman had learned that there was little leeway in Brother Terkelsen. He was a man who was utterly certain of his own rightness. Not that he was vain or cocky. It was simply that once he had made a decision he could not conceive of any other way being right. Because she understood him so well, she also knew that he would decide to proceed toward Sanpete. And because he led her husband around like a lamb on a string, he, and consequently the rest of them, would do whatever Terkelsen said to do, however foolish it was.

The woman knew that it was because of Terkelsen's careful planning and manipulating that they were all going to Sanpete. Yet how could she speak of this to her husband? It would do no good even to try. He was following Terkelsen because of his great faith or fanaticism or whatever it was, that he had been called by God to go. Therefore he went. And almost, she felt, the coming of President Buchanan's army was incidental. Yes, they had been ordered by Brigham Young to move south, though her husband tried to explain to her that it wasn't an order, simply counsel. But when Brigham spoke, everyone jumped, and to her that surely looked like an order.

Besides, they needn't have gone any farther south than Provo, for that was where the authorities had stopped. But not Brother Terkelsen. He had to continue on into Sanpete, and where he went the others must follow. It was purely a case of the blind leading the spineless.

Christian too would not look at her. The woman felt a stab of pity for this young man. He was a good boy, and very intelligent, but trying too hard to be something or somebody he wasn't. She had seen others like him, others trying to prove they were more than they were, others now pushing up grass from the underside of some lonely grave lost on a windswept hill.

She thought then of a story her father had told her as a little girl wanting too quickly to grow up. The story was of David the shepherd boy and his battle with the giant Goliath. The King wanted David to wear his armor, but when David, just a little lad, tried it on it had been too big and too ill-fitting. Promptly he removed it and then went on to greatness as himself. It didn't pay to try to be somebody else. Ever.

Maybe she should tell Christian that story. It surely seemed to her that he was running all over trying on every piece of strange armor he could find. Why couldn't he just be content to be himself? Would he listen to her? No, probably not, not in the mood he was in now. What Christian really needed was a good wife, someone who would settle him down and give him something worthwhile to live for.

Guilt then stirred within the woman, and she thought of what kind of wife she had been to Jens Jergensen. Why, oh why couldn't she love that man? She knew he cared for her, and perhaps he even loved her. At least he said he did often enough, and his kindness to her in so many little ways indicated that he meant it.

Yet deep within her the woman was suspicious. In so many ways her husband seemed far too good to be real. His ideals and attitudes were too lofty, his temper and patience too serene, and his general bearing toward others was altogether too meek and kind to come from what she thought of as a real man.

Once she had even tried to express this feeling to him, to explain her deep suspicions about the way he acted. He had merely smiled kindly at her, quoted some scripture or other, and then said that the Gospel of Jesus Christ made him the way he was. Talking with him was hopeless.

He seemed so sincere, so honest. Yet his every move smacked of either weakness or fanaticism. He was too easily ordered about, his voice was too quiet, the only thing he ever defended was his religion and that was done only in a meek way, and on and on. He just wasn't a man as her father had been. If they ever were attacked by Indians she could count on about as much help from him as she could from the baby girl she was nursing.

She was certain that one day she would see him break, that one day the pressures of life would become too great or else that one day he would just slip and reveal his true self. She was certain it would happen. The only reason it hadn't yet was because the situation hadn't been right. One day it would, though, and if she was still around she would have the last laugh. She surely would.

Unconsciously the woman looked down at Jens Jergensen's little daughter suckling contentedly at her breast. She was a beautiful little baby, and there was no denying how proud her father was of her. That much at least was real about him. Physically she knew that he was a strong man, but then again he was probably no stronger than any other normal adult. At least she had never seen him do anything that might prove his manhood. As the woman watched him slowly approach she found to her surprise that her heart was aching for him. For him and for herself as she suffered feelings of guilt, shame, and pity. Why on earth had she ever allowed herself to be married to him? And to have his baby? Oh God, why?

Look at him walking up, his eyes downcast, his hands in his pockets, his heavy old boots shuffling through the dirt. Where was his courage? Where was his strength? Why couldn't he be a man? Was there anything good she could say about him? Anything other than his infernal gentleness?

Well, maybe. One strength, if he had one at all, was his pure faith. That is if it really was faith. He seemed to be nothing else but a man of God. He acted as though he believed in his God implicitly. Ah, if she could only know of his sincerity. Or better yet, if she could only believe as he believed. He always seemed so happy, so . . . so content. It would be so nice to feel that way.

He had explained to her shortly after their marriage that most of his life he had spent going the ways of the world. That she could not imagine, but it was what he told her, and Kjersta had confirmed it.

Then, just a few years before, he had met two Mormon missionaries, and when their ways parted he was a new man. At first he had been skeptical of their new American faith with its prophets, modern revelation, polygamy, and so on.

But Jens Jergensen approached this problem as he did all others. He knelt down and simply asked God if this story the missionaries had told him was true. The woman supposed that it was because of his pure and simple faith, but when he had arisen from his knees tears were streaming down his face and he knew, nothing doubting, that Joseph Smith was indeed a prophet of God and that he, Jens Jergensen, must now be baptized in water and then give the rest of his life to serving God.

This service had first brought him and his devoted wife Kjersta across the Atlantic in a three-masted square-rigger to New Orleans, up the Mississippi in a stern-wheeler to St. Louis, and finally by wagon train across the plains to Great Salt Lake City, home of the Mormons. He was totally committed to living forever, as Christ wanted him to live, the fullness of the Gospel as he felt Mormonism taught it.

The woman knew she was no longer able to make such a personal commitment. It involved too much the giving of oneself to others. Somewhere they even had a scripture that said something about a man being able to serve God only so fast as he was willing to serve other people. According to that scripture both things were one and the same.

Well, that may be true, but the woman could not live it. Her own life had taught her that there was too much pain associated with loving others. To her it was a sacrifice in which the results were not worth the efforts. If she had ever had a testimony of the veracity of Mormonism it was gone now, lost somewhere in the bitterness of her own soul. It was not that she didn't believe. She just couldn't, wouldn't allow herself to care about it anymore.

Ever since she had been sealed to Jens it seemed that all he ever talked about was his eternal family. From the things he said, consciously and unconsciously, she knew how badly he had wanted children. His greatest fear had been that he might die without posterity.

He told her once that he felt that way because the Gospel taught him that as he was a child of God and so loved by Him, so he should have his own children and love and care for them. A man's life was such a short thing, he said, and when he was gone the only thing of value left behind was his family, his own children, raised by him to live the way they should, as honest hardworking people. Raising a good family was the most important thing a man could do in life. He had put it off too long, and it was time to be about it.

Day after day Jens Jergensen waited for word from either of his wives that one or the other of them was expecting a child, and when the word failed to come he did not seem discouraged about it at all. The woman of course knew that he was being foolish. Kjersta was certainly too old to have children, and in all likelihood he was also. One day she expressed herself to him about her doubts.

Quietly he had taken her by the shoulders and explained that she must not doubt, that it had been revealed to him by the spirit of God that he would yet be a father. Therefore, they must be patient until God, in His great wisdom, saw fit to act.

The woman said no more, and when a few weeks later she realized that both she and old Kjersta were pregnant she wasn't certain whether she was surprised or not. Certainly Jens was not. Instead of doing any of the things a man might do upon learning news of that nature he just smiled, took his wives by the hand, and dropped to his knees where he poured out his soul in thankfulness to his Father.

And there it was, the problem she was continually facing with this Jens Jergensen. Was he acting in a normal or acceptable manner? Was he really thanking God or was he still trying to impress the woman? Was he faithful, or was he fanatic? Honestly the woman did not know the answer.

With a start she realized that her husband was now standing patiently before her. For a long moment he regarded her closely, and then he spoke.

"Voman, ve have been in the canyon, but ve have found nothing that vould indicate vone vay or the other if there vere Indians there.

"But voman, if you say there vas an Indian, vell . . . , then there vas an Indian. You know much that ve do not, und so I believe you. The only thing is, I do not know vat ve do now. Brother Terkelsen says that ve must go on, Christian agrees, und I yust do not know vat to do."

For a moment the man stood lost in thought, and the woman again felt a stab of pity for this poor bumbling man.

"Voman, do you think there is real danger?"

He was simple and direct as he asked her, and suddenly the woman knew he would accept without question whatever she said. But just how was she to answer him?

The sun was sloping far to the west, a slight breeze ruffled the cottonwood leaves, and the woman could not imagine a more peaceful scene. Why was it that when one problem developed, it was certain to be followed by others that would only compound the first? First they had the Indians, and now their problems were compounding. Oh how she hated to tell them of it.

What exactly was a woman to do? Especially if she wasn't sure whether or not she even cared if they made it. That would surely be an easy way out. She could say nothing, do nothing. The men would blunder along as far as the Indians or the wagon would let them, and sometime prior to that she need simply walk away and vanish. It would be that easy, that certain, and who would ever know or even care? Certainly not her. The whole idea was perfect, just what she had been waiting for. So please explain why she was not going to do it.

"Jens, I saw an Indian, and I feel that there are others. If we were not in danger he would not have chased me. I fear they have seen Brother Terkelsen's stallion, and if they have we may rest assured they will stop at nothing to get it. Yes, there is danger, and I am afraid. Very afraid."

Awkwardly the big old Scandinavian stood there, a man unused to women and uncertain of their ways, wanting desperately to comfort this lady that he loved and yet not knowing just how to do it.

He'd met a man a year before, shortly after his sealing to the woman. The old man had told him how to be happy with his new wife.

"Women are like horses," he'd said. "Keep a strong hand on their bridle and pet 'em a mite and they'd stand up to most anything. Just let 'em get the bit in their teeth though and they'd make themselves miserable and their men too."

The view had shocked Jens Jergensen, and he had long thought of it. True it was that a man should be the head of his home, but to his way of thinking the woman counted too. His wife—no, wives—had walked beside him, never behind. When necessary he would lead out, but the women would be in agreement with his actions because they thought alike. That was part of eternal love.

He sensed now that they had come to a time when he would have to lead out, and he realized that he didn't know this woman well enough to be certain she thought the way he did. The woman, his woman, needed comfort and she needed it badly. But this was altogether a different proposition than comforting a horse. In a way he, Jens Jergensen, who feared no man or beast, was afraid of this woman. She was so knowing of things that he never even considered. And she was deep and mysterious too. Her thinking went way beyond his own simple ways. He knew that was at least part of the reason why he found it hard to believe that she could love him. Yet within his heart he hoped, oh how he hoped that she did.

Love was indeed a marvelous thing to consider, and constantly he prayed that the woman would learn to love him as he did her, for she was such a blessing in his life. And now to add to his blessings was the little daughter the Lord had given him and allowed him to keep. Could any man be more blessed?

Haltingly then he took the woman's face in his big hands and tenderly looked down into her eyes.

"Don't you vorry, voman. Don't you vorry. Ve go now, und ve go fast. Ve be closer to Uinta Springs, so ve vill go that vay. But ve vill go fast."

For a moment, just a very brief moment, the woman looked longingly into the deep blue of Jens Jergensen's eyes, and then with a shudder she turned aside.

"No we won't," was all she said, and her voice was so quiet that the man almost didn't hear her. But did it matter whether he heard her or not? The woman was certain that it didn't.

CHAPTER SIX

"Vat you say? Ve not go? Vy not, voman?"

Here it was, and the woman knew it. She could say nothing and just let everything take its course. Or she could speak up and accomplish absolutely nothing else except create dissension. She could not imagine that it would help their situation, not one bit. That would only happen if Jens, the only one who trusted her, would assume the leadership of the party. The woman knew the possibility of that occurring was so remote as to be non-existent. Jens Jergensen lead out? The thought might have been funny in any other situation. But not here. Not now.

Yet still they had a right to know while there was time to do something about it in safety. Or at least more safety than they would have if she left everything up to chance. So now the whole thing was on her shoulders. She, who cared little what happened to them. Oh if there was only one strong man in the group. How well her father could have handled this situation. Why, he would have . . .

"Voman, vat are you saying? Vy can ve not go on?"

"Because," and the woman sounded tired as she said it, "when the wagon got stuck in those rocks it broke out a felly on the wheel, and until that is fixed we won't be going very far at all."

Quickly Jens Jergensen strode to the wagon to survey the damage. Then he motioned for the others, out gathering up the stock, to come and look.

The woman walked up to them as they knelt near the wheel, and when Terkelsen had said everything he felt a need to say at such a time, the woman quietly spoke.

"Some decisions have to be made now, and I reckon we'd best be about it. Across the creek and beyond those trees is a long bench, and up there near the hill is a good place to camp.

"Jens, you should be able to find wood over there to repair the wheel, and if we brush out our tracks and take care we might get away with hiding there.

"Or," she continued, and she watched their faces carefully, for she was confident that this was their best chance, "we can abandon the wagon and walk back to Nephi. Then with a little help we can come back later for the wagon."

On Jens Terkelsen's face there was nothing but a look of pure astonishment, and it reflected in his voice.

"Vy should ve do that? Everything ve own is in the vagon, und if ve leave it ve vill be stolen blind. I say, ve don't leave it! Brother Jergensen vill fix it, und then ve vill go on. There is no danger here, ja, und no Indians either. I yust do not see vy ve get so upset by some dust only the voman saw."

Christian Kjerulf vigorously nodded his agreement. He was not so sure there weren't Indians, but he was sure as blue blazes not going to run from them. At the very worst they would only beg for food. He had seen that before, and he knew they were atrocious beggars. Fact is, he didn't think they should be given so much. If any of them ever asked him for food he'd sure as a double-barrel shotgun with both hammers back turn them down. He'd feed no lazy good-for-nothing Indians.

Besides, everything he needed to make his big stake in Sanpete was in that wagon, and he wasn't about to abandon it. Nosirree! He was for repairing and for moving on.

Only Jens Jergensen remained silent. He felt truly torn. He agreed with his woman that they should leave, but like the others he hated to abandon the wagon. In it was everything he owned, everything he would need to make the kind of home for his wife and daughter they should have.

"I think," he said, "that ve vill move the vagon up on the bench. Then ve vill make camp und I vill fix the vheel."

"Very good," agreed Jens Terkelsen. "I vill scout around for Indians again vile you drive the vagon over." He then looked hard at the woman. "That should satisfy anyvone, I vould say!"

With that he wheeled the red stallion and rode away.

For a moment the woman stood alone, and though the afternoon sun fell bright upon her she felt chilled. She was so lonely and so helpless. These men, these foolish men, had rejected the only ray of hope they had left. Why, oh why couldn't they see and understand?

Well, she could still leave. If she waited until dark and then just walked out she knew she could make it. But that idea had problems, one of which was the baby. How would Jens ever feed the child? When they got to Fort Ephraim he could always find a wet nurse, but he surely couldn't do that here in this desolate canyon. Maybe she should take the baby with her? But no, it was Jens's baby, not hers. If she walked off with it, Jens's life would end right there. He would be left with nothing to live for. No, she could not do that to any man, no matter what she thought of him personally. Right now her place was with him, and she had better reconcile herself to that. There was time enough to leave after they got to Fort Ephraim.

Calmly then she climbed into the wagon to place the baby in the little bed, and from there she climbed out onto the wagon seat.

Jens Jergensen geed the oxen over to the creek bank, where the woman helped brake the wagon down into the stream bed. They crossed and then nursed it up the other side, taking care lest some jolt destroy more fellies.

As the old oxen scrambled up the bank pulling the wagon behind them the felly broke completely loose and the two spokes it held swayed loose and fell to the ground. Christian Kjerulf, following behind and wiping out tracks with a tree bough as the woman directed, picked up the spokes and carried them into camp.

The wagon was halted two hundred yards farther on, shielded on one side by a thick aspen grove and on the other by a large outcropping of rock. The woman told her husband where to stop and then she too climbed down and began putting together a camp and fire.

Jens Jergensen watched her, amazed again at her ability and knowledge. The fire was small and built of dry wood, the aspen leaves would dissipate any smoke, and the outcropping of rock would shield them from observation. It was a good position, but as she explained, there were many such. All a person needed to do was keep his eyes open and know what he was looking for.

While Christian was sent up the hill with the ax to get a good piece of oak or serviceberry for the new felly, Jens Jergensen propped the wagon up and pulled the wheel off the axle, the well-greased cone or thimble slipping easily over the skane.

With skill born of long years of practice he removed the iron tire, and when Christian brought him a good piece of wood he began immediately to shape it with his ax and adze.

Far into the evening he worked, carefully planing it with a

spokeshave, and as he worked the others lounged near the small fire watching him.

The woman too watched, marveling at his skill and the care he showed in shaping the wood. This too was something new. She would have never guessed that he possessed such skill, and in spite of herself she was impressed. Jens Jergensen was building that felly to last, and the very solidness of his work seemed to give her hope. Perhaps they really would make it. Perhaps . . .

Lazily the small fire licked at the sticks Christian fed it, and the light flickered eerily on the spectral white trunks of the aspen, causing the shadows of the trees to leap and dance beyond them.

By day the mountains were an immense panorama spread out in magnificent disarray. To appreciate their vastness and beauty one had to be alone in them, somewhere along the hardbone ridges or snailing through the lonesome winding canyons.

With darkness a change came and distance was lost. The night brought a nearness that was at once intimate and frightening. At night one eagerly sought the warmth of a fire and the companionship of his own kind. It seems to be in the very nature of man to seek the strength of others when he is surrounded by the haunted blackness of the mountains.

So it was with the four Mormon pioneers. The inky darkness surrounding them bred a feeling of intimacy so strongly that they quietly shared thoughts they might otherwise have held to themselves.

"Do you think," Christian asked of no one in particular, "that Brother Brigham will let that dang army into the valley?"

"Vy surely he vill," replied Jens Terkelsen. "He vill not fight the whole United States."

"Then why in blue blazes did he fight them so hard last fall? If he was going to let them come in, how come he didn't save us all this trouble and do it then?"

"Christian," Jens Jergensen said, "President Young needed time. It is obvious that the Lord told him last fall to resist the army. He did, und now the Lord has told him to resist no longer but to move the Saints out of the valley und leave the rest up to Him. Ja, und that is vat ve are doing. Ve know not vether ve vill ever return, but no matter. This is the Lord's Church, ve are the Lord's people, und Brigham Young vill be our Prophet und our governor yust as long as the Lord vishes it to be so. Ve must trust in Him und let Him do vith us as He vill."

"Yeh, I reckon that's about what we are doing. Thing is, why is that blasted armed mob coming here anyhow? Mormons are mostly quieter than a hole in the ground. Fact is, we're so quiet we'll let Cumming or any other Gentile call himself governor if he wants, as long as he lets us alone. I heard they said we were treasonous, but shucks, that just ain't so. We're only prophetic is all, and if the United States don't repent they *will* be destroyed! I've heard Brigham Young say so, and he said he'd heard Joseph Smith say so too. And when that happens, by thunder, then it won't matter who they send here for governor! The Kindgom will be in charge then!"

They all chuckled at Christian's vehemence, and that served only to get him more upset.

"Why in blue blazes is everybody laughing? It's so and you all know it. I ain't seen everything, but I've seen and heard enough to know that the United States has been meaner to us than a hydrophoby skunk would have been. There was trouble in New York, mobs in Kirtland, more mobs in Independence, Far West, and Diahman, murder at Haun's Mill, Nauvoo, and Carthage, and never once has the blasted government stepped in to see justice done. Fact is, sometimes they've even been behind our troubles."

"Vat you say is true, Christian, und ve vill not argue, though none of us here have seen any of that trouble. But you should know that the government has not been all bad."

"Oh yeh, when weren't they?"

"Vell, ven they paid the vay for five hundred of our men to go vest vith the battalion. Vithout that money und that food und so on ve might have been in great trouble."

"First time I ever heard the battalion called a good thing," muttered Christian.

"Ja, maybe so, but it vas, und if you vill look at it you vill know vat I mean. The United States did not yust call out the battalion for no reason. I vas told that President Young offered the services of two thousand of our brethren to the government so that ve could be paid for going vest. Vell, the government did not do that, but they did offer to hire five hundred men as soldiers for use in the var vith Mexico, und that vas on the vay vest. Ja, it vas a great economic blessing to our people, even if it vas a difficult blessing to earn."

"Well, you may be right. I don't know. But even if you are, that still don't excuse this government mob that is coming to destroy us now."

"Ja, that is true, but have faith. The Lord vill care for us."

"If that is so," asked the woman, breaking her silence for the first time, "then why didn't the Lord stop the army before we had to abandon our homes? Seems to me if He really loved this people he ought to make it a little easier on them."

"Voman," her husband replied, "ven did the Lord ever make it easy for His people? He has told us that trials yust make us stronger. Besides, you forget that God did stop the army this past vinter vith all the snow und cold veather. He could do it again if He chose, but He vill not take avay the freedom of a man to do as he vants, nor of a whole nation either. If the army chooses to try to destroy the Saints or drive them permanently from their homes, then God vill use that as a judgment against them.

"Ve must never forget that ve are members of the Kingdom of God. The Prophet Daniel said that vhen God set up His Kingdom in the last days it vould never be destroyed, but vould roll forth und destroy all other nations. Und I know that is yust vat it vill do! The Lord vill let the Gentiles become yust so vicked, und then they vill be destroyed. That, Christian, vas vat President Young und Joseph Smith vere speaking of.

"Ja, I have heard many say, und by golly I feel it myself, that this army vill be the last indignity the Lord vill allow His people to suffer. The vorld is ripe with iniquity, sin, und injustice, und it yust may be that this is the final straw that vill bring the Lord in His glory to destroy the vicked from off the face of the earth. Then vill the Kingdom of God roll forth to rule the earth in righteousness und glory, und ve vill all be part of the great millennial reign of Christ."

"Yeh," agreed Christian. "We've been hearing that the Second Coming is close. Maybe this is it. Maybe it is."

"Ja," said Jens Terkelsen, "it yust might be. But ve have been told so many times that it vas close that I am beginning to vonder yust vat close means. Brother Brigham von't say for sure ven it vill be, und you can bet that I vill not hold my breath vhile I am vaiting."

"Brother Terkelsen, you know that the scripture says no man knows the day or the hour, und I suspect that vill include the Prophet too. Still, all the signs seem to say that is is near, und I am doing my best to prepare for it. Perhaps it vill not come before I die, but because I have tried to prepare myself I vill alvays be ready no matter vhat may come, vether it vill be the Second Coming, death, or hopefully yust a long und happy life vith my family. Ja, it is not so important ven it happens as it is that ve vill all be ready.

"Until then, it vill be up to us to push forward the Kingdom und the Gospel, und ve can do that only if ve are vorthy und righteous. So ve must get ready. That, as I see it, is the main message of the prophets."

For a few moments all were silent, and the only sounds in camp were the crackling fire and the methodical scraping of the spokeshave. Once the red stallion nickered into the darkness, but there was no reply, and in a moment he returned to cropping grass.

"I heard back in Nephi," again ventured Christian, "that the Utes have killed twenty-four of the Saints since they first came, back in '47."

"Ja," agreed Jens Terkelsen, "und that does not count Captain Gunnison und the eleven others vith him."

"Thirty-six."

"Ja, it is a lot, for sure."

There was silence for a few moments, and the thinking was mostly of the same thing. The darkness seemed to all of them just a little blacker and more threatening and the fire just a little cheerier.

"And do you know," continued Christian, "that seven of them were killed over in Sanpete Valley? Or that four of those seven were killed at Uinta Springs, where we should be right now?"

"Und I heard," added Terkelsen, "that they found the three of them right off, but the fourth they didn't find for two days."

"How come do you think it took 'em so long to find that one?"

"Vell, he vas cut up something awful, und then the Indians buried him under the load of flour he vas carrying, right in his own vagon. It vas a mess too, ven they finally did find him."

"How come do you think them savages cut folks up so bad? We ain't done them no harm for 'em to act like that."

"That is the big question, boy. Vy do they do it? Vy do they do it at all ven ve are supposed to be at peace vith them?"

"Some say," said Jens Jergensen, "that they are afraid of losing their land. But from vat I hear the Indian has no concept of land ownership as ve do. My guess vould be that they fight because our cultures clash. Ours says peace, und theirs says war. It is yust the thing to do. Then too, there are no doubt some vhite people who have given them good reason for fighting."

"Like what?"

"Vell, some say that the only good Indian is a dead vone, und they try to make all Indians good. That vould be unjustified killing, und I suspect that vould make anyvone unhappy, even an Indian."

The others were surprised at this view, and even the woman was startled to hear this perception of the Indian problem. Her father had often expressed the same thing, only she had to admit it had not been expressed in such an educated way as this Mormon had just expressed it.

"Well, I'm powerful glad," breathed Christian, "that we are at peace with them savages now." He glanced again out into the darkness, made even blacker by his staring into the fire, and then continued.

"It's so blasted dark out there it'd take a feller both hands just to find his nose. Sitting here with no guns and maybe Indians all over makes me feel kinda like an old hen at a coyote convention, if you know what I mean. In fact, I'm about as nervous as a centipede with the chilblains."

Both older men chuckled at Christian's comments, and the woman even found herself smiling. But after a moment there was silence again, and over the crackling of the fire they could hear the water from the spring above them splashing along its rocky course toward Salt Creek.

Far off a lonesome coyote yipped its complaints to the sky, and then the night was still.

"We had a man, a mighty fine man, name of Benjamin Franklin," the woman said. "He helped out a lot when our country was just getting started. He once said something that's made a lot of sense to me, and I've thought often of it, trying to understand. He said: 'Savages we call them, because their manners differ from ours, which we think the perfection of civility. They think the same of theirs.'"

There was total silence then, silence while they digested what she had said. Then with an explosion of breath Christian Kjerulf angrily spoke.

"Does that mean that you go along with the murderous treachery of these red-skinned beggars?"

"Christian, you did not understand what I said. I don't know for sure how I feel. I am, well, I am only trying to understand them. My father fought them nearly his whole life, yet he said that they were a good people and that a man could learn a lot from them. He learned, and he taught me some of what they taught him. He respected them."

"Well, by thunder I don't," growled young Christian. "They're murdering dogs, every last one of them, and ought to be treated as such! That's what I say!"

"Vell then," quietly replied Jens Jergensen, "you are mistaken, und you do not believe in Mormonism."

"What?"

"Do you not remember vat it says in the Book of Mormon, that the Indian is descended from the House of Israel, just as you are?"

"Yeah, but . . ."

"No buts, my son. This is truth, und you listen to me. The first ancestor of the Indians vas Laman, son of Lehi, the Prophet, who vas driven from Jerusalem ven Zedekiah vas king, six hundred years before Christ.

"Laman vas deceived by Satan and so rebelled against his family. Und so God cursed him und his descendants vith a dark skin. Und so ve have the Indians. Yust as much our brothers as anyvone else.

"Mostly since that day they have been a vicked und idolatrous people, but the Book of Mormon says, too, that vone day they vill repent und become fair-skinned as any of us.

"That is vy Brother Brigham tells us to be friends vith the Lamanite or Indian. He says that if a vhite man steals, shoot him, but if an Indian steals, teach him better.

"That is vat I believe too, und it is vone reason vy I carry no guns. I vill soon have him to be my neighbor, und my great desire is to teach him of his great heritage, to tell him that he too is a child of God und a brother to all of us. But you tell me, how can I teach him if I am shooting the gun at him or even pointing it his vay? Vat a fine vay to teach of love."

"Well, all that sounds mighty noble, Brother Jergensen. Still, I'd bet a new rifle you'd fight them if they attacked your wife or daughter."

"Ja, Christian, I suppose I vould. You see, a man has the responsibility to defend that vich is his, und I am first of all a man vith a family. Und then I am secondly a good neighbor to the Indians. But after I vas done fighting him I vould help him up und then teach him better."

"You're certain it would be you on top?" grinned Christian.

"Ja, I vould be if I vas defending my voman or my daughter."

It was said simply and with no boasting, yet Christian and the others suddenly knew that the old man meant what he said.

The woman too wondered, but her wondering was spiced with doubt. This old man had never seen an Indian fight. Furthermore, he had probably never fought himself. He surely did have a lot to learn.

"Vone other thought, Christian. You feel as you do toward the Indians und say in your heart that you are right. Because they do not believe as you nor act as you, they are therefore less human than you und deserve to be treated that vay.

"Then in the next breath you utter oaths against the mobbers, as you call them, who are even now marching under the flag of the United States to drive us from our vonderful homes und valleys und perhaps destroy us also.

"Do you not understand, Christian, that the people of the United States, the Gentiles as ve call them, feel toward us exactly as you feel toward the Lamanites, und for precisely the same reasons? They yust do not understand vat ve believe, und because of that lack of understanding, they vant to use up und destroy. They have been told falsehoods about us, und they have not taken the time to see if all they heard vas true. Thus they vant to kill us all if ve vill not become as they are.

"Because ve vill not, ve now have trouble. Last vinter ve fought them, und God fought them too, und because of our victories ve vere given a whole vinter to prepare our minds und our bodies for this time. Und now ve give up our homes und ve flee again, hopefully only to Sanpete, but perhaps much farther.

"Tell me, Christian. You have a good heart, und you know right from wrong. Do you honestly vish the Indians to suffer as the Mormons have done? Ven ve act as you suggest, do you blame our red brothers for treating us as enemies?"

When Christian didn't answer, Jens Jergensen stood and walked to where the wheel lay, and inserting the two spokes into the hub and then into his new felly he placed it in position, driving in wedges to hold it in place.

"Tomorrow," he said, "ve vill heat the iron tire und then by golly ve vill be on our vay."

He straightened then and walked back to the fire. It was late, but he felt a reluctance to retire. There was a peace here, a closeness that he thoroughly enjoyed and yet felt only rarely. It seemed to him that if they all went to bed they would lose that feeling and it might never return.

Ja, if a man could only know what was in the heart of another, or of a woman. Kjersta, now, had been easy for him to understand. Like him she had always been simple and open, giving her life each day to ensure his happiness. The woman, though, was different. Perhaps it was because she was so much younger, or maybe it was because she had not come from the old country. Still, she was his wife, and to him it seemed but right that she share with him her thoughts and feelings. He did with her, or at least he did mostly. There were a few things, but, well, they were so long ago and so far away.

But the woman's feelings were different. They were of right now, of him and of his daughter, and though she had said nothing old Jens was certain they were not good. It was not anything definite, but there were times when he was certain she looked at him with loathing and disgust.

True it was that those looks of hers opened the wells of anger he held buried deep within him, but never yet had he allowed the flood to surface. It was simply not right that a man should show anger to his wife, the woman he loved. It was neither manly nor Christ-like, and so he held himself still. Often he had thought, though, and surprisingly too, that it was amazing how a man could get more angry with the ones he loved than he ever could with others. He supposed the reason for that was simply because loved ones counted more than others did. At least he was certain that was the reason he reacted as he did.

Many, many prayers had he offered to God because of the coldness and bitterness he felt from his wife. At first he had prayed for wisdom and understanding so he might be able to make her happy. Lately though he had prayed more for her, for he felt, and he shuddered as he thought of it, the thought was so abominable, that the woman, his woman, even hated the little child, the little spirit who had come so recently from the presence of God Himself. Oh, how Jens Jergensen wanted to be wrong about that. But from the things she said, little things that might have had no meaning, and from the way the woman looked at the baby, he was certain he was right.

So he prayed, prayed with all his heart and soul, that he be given the solution to the problem, that he be told how to teach his wife, the woman he loved, of the true and correct path of eternal happiness.

But the heavens seemed as brass and he could get no answer. How could he teach her, a woman so inwardly turned and deeply buried in her past, that only by love, by gentleness, and by service to others could one find happiness and freedom from the haunted specters of a guilty and sorrowful memory? ✓

There had to be a way, but as yet God had not revealed that way to Jens Jergensen. He seemed to say only, "Peace, my son. Be still and wait and you shall see the wisdom of God unfold."

So Jens waited, and as he waited he cried in his heart at the torture and anguish the woman he loved was suffering. How could he, the one God had sealed to her as her husband, head, and helpmeet, add to her sorrows by angry accusations and denunciations?

Ja, he could not be a true man and do so! His only course must be one of love and kindness and gentleness. That had been the way of Christ. It must be the way of any true man, any Latter-day Saint priesthood holder. It must be his way. Of course at times it was hard, but Jens Jergensen knew in his heart that one day all would be well with all of his family. He knew, for he had the promise, by the whisperings of the Spirit, from God.

"Voman, it is late, und I think it best ve retire. Ve have vone big day tomorrow. Vat you say?"

All agreed, and shortly the camp was still, the fire little more than a glowing red eye in the darkness. An owl hooted from a nearby tree, and a fieldmouse cowered at the sound, then sniffed curiously at the sleeping camp.

Up the hill a breeze ruffled the aspen leaves and the owl took off on lazy wings through the dark aisles of the trees. The mouse, relieved, moved hesitantly from the shelter of a rock, circled the small camp, and disappeared on some nocturnal business of its own. A bat poised, fluttering dark wings in the air above them, then swooped off, and there was no other sound but the gurgling water and some of the livestock cropping grass.

A long time later, in the darkest hour before dawn, and far up on the hill, sound suddenly seemed to hesitate, and then for a moment there was absolute silence. The red stallion's head came up alertly and the woman opened her eyes and lay still, listening.

Something . . . no, *somebody,* was out there, and the woman knew it.

CHAPTER SEVEN

In the hour before dawn there is less light than at any other time of the night, making it the least likely time to move about. Yet in the darkness of that hour Hoskoots came down off the hill with all the leaping stealth of a hunting mountain lion. He moved quickly through the trees and brush, yet not a twig snapped nor pebble rolled beneath his feet. His course, despite the darkness, was true.

Most Indians were good stalkers, for their lives depended upon their ability. But where most were simply good, Hoskoots was a master of the art. He differed also from his dark-skinned brethren because he enjoyed working at night. To him the darkness was security, just that much more covering under which he might accomplish his nefarious deeds.

So now Hoskoots, the Ugly One, slipped down the slope. His moccasins moved through the heavy ground cover and over the thick carpeting of discarded pine needles like a shadow, yet while he ran he cursed viciously in his mind.

Hoskoots was angry, terribly angry. He didn't bother to wonder whether he was angry with himself or with the Mormonees. He was just angry, and that was certain.

He had been tricked. He, Hoskoots, the master reader of sign, had been tricked by these, these white people. It was a terrible blow to the ego.

He had spent most of the afternoon and night looking for them, riding clear to Uinta Springs and back, but his efforts brought no results at all. Not a wagon, not a fire, not even tracks, and that did bother him. Everything left tracks. Everything.

It had been after dark before he found where the wagon entered the creek, but he never did find where they emerged.

Hours of futile searching behind him and with absolutely no results to his credit, Hoskoots had decided that they were gone and that he would never see them again. The thought had even crossed his mind that they might have been spirits. That thought set him back a little, and he was about ready to find a place to bed down when he saw far below him through the trees the dull red eye of what must be a fire.

The flickering light was visible for only an instant, but Hoskoots thought about spirits no longer. At least not then. He had been led to the place of the Mormonee camp, and now he must do the rest.

Leaving his pony he crept quickly down the hill, slowing his descent only when he neared the camp. Here the Ute became more wary, for there was something that bothered him about the situation.

Whoever had chosen this site had known what he was doing. It was hidden from every angle, had water close by, and the tracks leading to it had been obliterated.

Suddenly he paused. Could that mean the people of the camp did know about him? He recalled his blunder of the afternoon previous. It was certainly possible that they had seen him. And suppose he was right? Could this silent place then be a trap?

Right then the Ute almost turned back. But the red stallion snorted a little, he got hold of himself, and he moved again toward the camp. How could they possibly know? If they did they would have chased him. No, they couldn't know! It was simply that they had been cautious while he had been deceived.

Why, even if they did know of him that was a good thing. It meant that they had feared to ride after him. The Mormonees afraid of one Ute warrior. Hah! His chest swelled a little at the thought.

Hoskoots at last reached the edge of the clearing, and here he paused. Secretly he was vastly pleased with his approach. He had made absolutely no noise as he slipped down the hill. Of course he knew that there were situations or events in his approach that might give him away. For one thing, he had interrupted the chirping of the crickets as he passed, and an expert could have perceived that difference. Yet who beside himself was expert enough to have noticed that? No one. It was a thing not worth worrying about.

Carefully he surveyed the sleeping camp. The fire was just a pile of glowing embers which came to life only as sporadic breezes fanned up a tiny flame. The cattle and goats were secured within a rope corral, and the wagon stood tall and silent in the muted darkness.

Still probing, the eyes of Hoskoots at last found what they were seeking. His red stallion stood tethered to the wagon wheel. But his head was up and he was watching the Ute intently.

He was a good horse, that one. Hoskoots knew he must be careful or the animal might betray him. Yet there was little time for care. Too little, for dawn was fast approaching.

For long moments he crouched, absolutely still. But there was nothing. No sound or movement at all. Wait a moment. Yes. Yes, there was a sound. Intermittently he could hear the soft noises of sleep coming from beneath the wagon, the snoring of a man lost in the depths of slumber.

Satisfied now that all was well the Ute crept across the clearing toward the red horse, his razor-sharp knife in his hand to sever the rope that held the animal bound.

At last he reached the animal, and it made no sound save to toss its head just a little. Up close the horse was even more magnificent than he had supposed. Oh, how the spirits were smiling upon Hoskoots!

He raised his knife to sever the rope and was just at the point of doing so when he saw, out of the corner of his eye, the dull gleam of firelight on metal, and it moved!

Hoskoots froze, and as he did so he involuntarily sucked in his breath and held it.

"Was I you," a woman's voice spoke quietly, "I'd lower that knife and skedaddle on out of here. I surely would. Else I'll blow a hole in you so big the stars'll shine through it."

Hoskoots stood perfectly still. Overhead the black sky glittered with the tiny lanterns of a million stars, and the serrated ridge down which he had so recently come beckoned longingly up into the darkness. A pocket of pitch long imprisoned in an old log popped with a sudden explosion as the heat from the fire finally located and freed it, and Hoskoots jerked in fear at the sound.

Overhead the aspen leaves rustled fitfully as a wandering canyon breeze stirred them to action, and the water of the tiny stream gurgled over a small stone and eddied out of the slack water behind it, and the Ute liked the sound of it.

Suddenly Hoskoots realized how very much he enjoyed these little things he took for granted. Though he understood only part of what the woman had said to him, he could see the gleam of the rifle in her hand and he knew that he was only seconds away from death.

For an instant he thought of Chipetz, the beautiful little squaw that so often filled his mind, and then he snapped back to reality.

How had this happened to him? How could a woman, a white squaw, know enough to catch him as this woman had done?

The mind of Hoskoots raced, and the seconds seemed like hours as he waited for the explosion of the rifle.

His limbs began to cramp, and he suddenly realized that he was holding his breath. He desperately wanted to turn so he could face her.

No! No, he didn't want to face her. He wanted only to run, to get as far away from this woman as he could. She was bad medicine. Very bad medicine. Why had the spirits, so friendly to him, brought him into such an awful position?

Maybe it was the red stallion. Perhaps it was not a horse after all. Perhaps it too was a spirit. Why certainly, that must be it. The woman and the horse were spirits. And so were the men and the wagon. That was why they left no tracks! Spirits left no tracks!

That was it! Why . . .

"Em-pi-queay!"

Hoskoots stood transfixed. He was so amazed that he actually started to turn to look at this woman before he realized what he was doing and turned back.

He knew now, nothing doubting, that he was right. This was a spirit camp. It had to be. For this woman had, out of the darkness and in a quiet steady voice, spoken his own tongue.

But even more impossible than that was what she had said. He could not believe that he had heard her right, yet the sound of her voice was still ringing in his ears.

Suddenly she spoke again, and this time he knew.

"Em-pi-queay, ahp! You go, now!"

Hoskoots waited no longer, but without a backward glance fled the camp at a dead run, and he didn't stop until he reached his pony far up on the hill.

He must return to his encampment. The others, the wise ones, must know of this.

CHAPTER EIGHT

Slowly the woman let out her breath, but she didn't move until the red stallion finally dropped his muzzle and began cropping the thick grass again.

At last she laid down the stick she had been holding and placed the knife that had given the metallic gleam to her "rifle" back in its scabbard.

She was shaking from head to foot, and her whole body was bathed in a cold sweat. For the moment, though, she was satisfied. She had done it. She had actually scared away that Indian. It had been risky, but now she felt it had been worth it. If only . . .

"Voman, that vas very brave."

The woman shrieked and spun around, so unexpectedly had her husband spoken to her. But then as she realized who it was she fled into his arms and clung to him sobbing as he softly stroked her head.

As her sobbing subsided the woman found her head swimming with question after unanswered question. How long had Jens been standing there? Had he too heard the approach of the Ute? He held a knife in his hand. Would he have used it? And then there was the biggest question of all. If he had heard the approach of the Indian, and if he had been standing there armed, why hadn't he taken the man's part and driven the Ute away instead of leaving it all up to her?

There was only one answer, an answer so obvious it made her feel sick and ashamed all at the same time, sick that she had married him and ashamed that there could be such a spineless man anywhere. Anywhere at all.

He had told her he would fight for her, and oh heavens how she had wanted to believe him. He seemed so sincere, so forthright. And she had learned many good things about him during this journey. But all of the good in the world paled into insignificance when placed alongside such cowardice as he possessed. She could never respect this man, could never expect any kind of help from him when it mattered most. Suddenly her decision was made and the weeks and months of helpless and frustrated waiting were over. Now was the time to talk, to tell this man, this strange and far too gentle Mormon, of her feelings. It was a difficult thing to speak of, yet the guilt and uncertainty she had experienced, mixed with the distaste she now felt, compelled her to try.

She pulled from his arms, then, and walked to the fire. With a small stick she stirred it to life and added a small amount of fuel, for in the pre-dawn darkness she felt suddenly chilled.

"How . . . how long were you standing there?"

"Not too long. Ja, but I heard, und I vas proud. Courage is a rare thing, und I am happy my daughter vill learn it from you."

Bitterly the woman looked at him in agreement. Yes, the little girl would learn it from her, but that was the only place she would get courage from. And precious little good that would do her if she was raised by this man.

"Jens?"

"Ja, voman?"

"Jens, I must talk to you. I have some feelings, and I think I'd better express them. Something is wrong with our marriage, very wrong. I simply cannot love Kjersta's baby! And Jens, I feel the same way about you, only worse, and . . .

"Oh, I wish I could explain this better. Sometimes I am so confused.

"Jens, you say the Church is true, but I don't know that! You seem to be deeply religious, but I question whether your religion is good or whether it is fanaticism. Of course I really don't know which it is, but from all I see you seem to show the weaknesses of a fanatic. Do you see what I mean about being confused?"

The man Jens Jergensen stood in stunned silence. What she said hurt, it hurt deeply, but perhaps this was best. At least it was finally getting out in the open. He wanted desperately to say something though, yet still he kept silent. Somehow he must encourage the woman to continue, to share with him all these pent-up feelings.

"Jens, are you angry?"

"No . . . I am not angry. Vat is there that I should be angry about? You must say vat you feel."

"Oh, Jens, I am so lost and so frightened. In some ways I envy even you. For you life seems so simple, so direct. Everything in your life has a rule. You seem to have only to follow the rules and you are entirely happy.

"But Jens, nothing is really like that. There is no such thing as an easy answer. And the only rules I have found lead to unhappiness and misery. It has all happened before, and I can see that it is all in the process of happening again."

"Voman, I don't know that I understand . . ."

"Of course you don't, and I'm not certain that I really want you to. You see the whole world through colored glass, and I don't know that I really want to break it."

"But voman . . . ?"

"Jens, you must listen. I have to tell you now. I have to be fair with you as well as being fair with myself. To leave this unsaid would only make it worse for both of us.

"Jens, I don't love you. I never have, and I never will. This is partly because I can't, but mostly I guess because I won't. I was sealed to you because my father told me it was right, but I see now that he was wrong. I never should have done it. Jens, I won't allow myself to love anyone, ever again.

"You ask why? I will tell you why. Whenever I have loved someone they have been cruelly taken from me, and I can't stand ever again to bear the pain that comes from that. Death is too awful and too permanent and I can't bear it. I won't bear it."

"Voman . . ."

"No, wait a moment and let me finish. I know how harsh and awful it sounds to say that I don't love or want that sweet little baby girl. But Jens, can't you see how I feel? As surely as I let myself love her she will die. I know as surely as I am standing here now that it will happen, and I couldn't stand to go through that kind of pain again.

"My father, mother, brothers and my own little son lie moldering in the ground, and I can't, no I won't let myself feel and love, ever again! The specter of death has haunted me enough in my life, and I will never give it another chance to gain a victory over me. I'm sorry, Jens, but that is how I feel."

"Ja, voman, if only I had known," Jens said softly. "I have neglected my duty in teaching you the Gospel. All your sorrows vould be gone if you but understand the love Jesus Christ has for you and the sacrifice He made in your behalf."

"Jens, don't start preaching to me. Not now!"

"Ja, voman, I vill preach no sermon, not if that is your vish. But I yust vant you to know, by golly, that vone need never fear death. Not since the resurrection of Christ. All vill rise from the dead, for He has so promised. That is vy the Apostle Paul said, 'O death, vhere is thy sting? Oh grave, vhere is thy victory?' Ja, it hurts to lose those ve love. It is a lonely, lonely feeling. But because of Christ ve can be comforted. That is vat the Gospel of Jesus Christ is all about."

Jens stopped speaking, for he realized that the woman was wearing that faraway look she wore when she was living within herself. She had heard nothing he'd said, and his heart ached as he thought of the sorrow and pain she must still be experiencing. If only she could feel, could understand. The Gospel was the only thing that had brought comfort to his own soul, and he knew it would to hers if she would but give it the chance.

He thought again of what she had said, of not loving either him or his child. Was that possible? That thought hurt as much as anything, and he felt a need to pursue it. He somehow needed to get on more firm ground where he might help this woman he loved.

"Voman, are you listening to me?"

"Umph."

"Voman, if all that you say is true, vy did you marry me? Vy did you consent to bear my child?"

"I don't know, Jens. I just don't know. A thousand times I have asked myself that same question. It has never been answered to my satisfaction.

"Maybe I was lonely, and maybe I was just trying to be obedient to my father. I have wondered that. Even at the time I was surprised that I should say yes to you. I seriously thought of saying no, and now with all my heart I wish I had."

She paused for a moment to stare into the sky. It was slowly graying in the east as the bright stars of night faded from sight. How she wished she could just fade away as they did. It would all be so much easier, so much better than this.

"Maybe, Jens, the whole thing might have worked out if it hadn't been for my baby. If only he hadn't died . . . if only I wasn't expected to love another as my own.

"But Jens, a baby is too real, too much a part of a woman's body to not involve love, a love that I am not willing to give. A baby is a living symbol of the love a man and woman feel for each other. A baby is, as you once said, the living continuation of a man and a woman, something that will speak for all generations of their infinite affection for each other."

"Ja, voman, und so our little daughter is all that you have said."

"No, Jens. No, she isn't! For you perhaps that is true, but how can it be for me when I have no feeling of love, of attachment for the little child or for her father."

"You . . . you have no feelings at all for me?"

Desperately the woman struggled with her emotions as well as her answer. This was crazy, but now that she was saying these things she found herself wondering if she really meant them.

It was true that she didn't feel for Jens Jergensen the things she had always wanted to feel for a husband. But even if she didn't, then what of the things she did feel for him? Was there only one kind of love, only one way to love a man? All along she had looked on his quietness and gentleness as signs of weakness. But suddenly another thought struck her. All her life she had lived with her father, a man who was loud and boisterous, a man who even enjoyed violence. But Jens was different, and it suddenly came to her that his very quietness and gentleness gave her a feeling of peace that she had never before experienced. Could she be wrong? Might there be a chance for them?

No! She must not think of that! It would be better this way, to sever everything. Only by doing that could she protect herself from the mental and emotional anguish she had suffered in the past. Her answer, now that she had come this far, must be firm and strong. She must not waiver!

"No, I have no feelings. None at all. Unless perhaps they are sorrow and pity and much, much regret."

"Voman, you do not know vat you are saying. You can't know . . ."

"Jens, I know very well what I am saying, and I will be as fair with you as I can. The baby girl is yours and you must keep her. When we get to Fort Ephraim you can find a wet nurse for her and I will return. I cannot bear to burden either of our lives any further."

Now the big old Scandinavian Saint was truly stunned. This was more than he had bargained for. Much, much more than he had imagined she would say.

His woman, his beloved wife, not love him?

Impossible! Not after what they had shared with each other. Jens

Jergensen knew how he felt about the woman. He had loved her since the day of their sealing, and he was not about to let her walk away now. He could not live without her.

Then too, he had his daughter to consider. What kind of a life could he alone provide for a little baby girl? It would be a very poor life, and he knew it, knew it with all his heart.

No, she would not go! This woman was his, sealed to him by one who held the authority to do so. They were bound together for all eternity, and she didn't understand that. If she did, then she would feel different. Somehow he must explain, he must make her understand the solid and eternal nature of their marriage and of their family unit.

"Voman, I think because of your fright from the Indian you say these things. Und I understand that you are upset. That is vy you say things that you do not, cannot mean."

"Oh, Jens, why can't I make you see that I do mean them, that I am right?"

Jens turned and walked away from the woman, his fists clenched so tightly that his knuckles were white, doing his best to keep quiet.

No, by golly, the time for being quiet, the time for being the gentleman, was past! Ja, he must now exert the authority that God had given him as the husband of this woman! It was his responsibility to help her get her thinking in the right place. If he didn't try, then he would be as wrong as she was.

Turning he strode quickly back to where the woman sat by the fire. Taking her by the arms he pulled her to her feet and peering keenly into her eyes he spoke with all the force and power of his deep-set convictions, his voice low and yet intensely powerful.

"Now, voman, hush und listen to your husband, und I vill tell you vat you need to know."

Instantly the woman realized that there was something new about her husband's voice, a firmness that she had never heard before. Yet surprisingly it was a firmness intermingled with such gentleness that at first she wondered if perhaps she might be mistaken.

Yet there was something, just enough of something different, that it caused the woman to listen to the man Jens Jergensen, really listen, for perhaps the first time since she had known him. There was a strength in his voice, something so different that she even wondered if she might have been wrong about his being a coward. Could he perhaps be more of a man, worthy of more respect than she had shown him heretofore? This was certainly not the Jens Jergensen she had known up to a few moments ago, and she felt a little tingle as he spoke.

"Voman, all my life I have prayed to God that he vould bring me a child. For fifty years I have patiently vaited, most of that time with Kjersta, preparing myself as best I could to vone day become a good father.

"Finally the Good Lord saw fit to bring us you, und to you Kjersta und I have given our hearts und souls. For you ve vould do about anything, und you know that is true. My heart vas expanded to love two vomen and not yust vone.

"Und then to us comes a son und a daughter, und the Lord expands my heart vith more love than I ever thought possible. Now I can love two children as much as I loved yust you and Kjersta before the little vones vere born. That is a great miracle, und I thank God for it.

"Voman, ven vone loves another then that means to me that he must forget himself. Selfishness has no place in love, for vat selfish person ever thought more of someone else than he did of himself? How then, I ask you, could a selfish person ever love? You see, he could not. It vould be impossible.

"Voman, I love you! Und I show it, or try to, by being gentle und polite vith you. Ja, at times it vould be easy to quarrel und fight vith you, for often I do not agree vith vat you say und do. But vould that be a good vay to show love? No, nor vould it be a Christ-like vay to act! So I don't act that vay.

"But now you have made a great mistake. I have seen it in your eyes, und I have heard it in your voice. You have mistaken how I express my love to you as a veakness, und because of that you say that I am less than a man. Me, Jens Jergensen, who has come so close to killing a man vith these bare hands that even now I shudder to think of it, less than a man. You think to yourself that a man can only be so if he is loud und a braggart, violent in nature, und so on. I myself have been that vay, und I say that you are wrong. Ja, my heart cries to think of vat you have thought of me.

"Und furthermore, because I try to be kind to my friend Jens Terkelsen, tolerant of his problems and gentle in my speech to him, it is in your mind that I am veak again und that he drags me here und there at his vill.

"Ja, und I know that he thinks so too. But voman, use your head.

Do you suppose I vould allow my vife, daughter, und myself to be moved to a new home if I had any doubts that it vas a good thing?

"Und vone thing more. Vat kind of a friend vould a man be if he could not bear to help his friends to feel strong and successful? Ja, he vould be no friend at all. By allowing Brother Terkelsen to be head of the party I help him to feel good und successful. Vith young Christian I do the same thing by asking for his advice. I think I could not be a good friend und do othervise.

"Besides, voman, vat else has poor Brother Terkelsen got? I have been blessed vith good vives und fine children vile he must remain alone in the vorld. Do you not see that a man must lead out und have success in something to be happy? So this thing I give to Brother Terkelsen, as his friend, for his happiness.

"Ja, but still it hurts to have the vone I love see this my gift of love as a veakness. Voman, I vill not try to hide from you that sometimes it has been hard to keep from showing you vat I am truly like. Ja, sometimes ven I am hurt it vould be very easy to forget that God vould have me always be the gentleman to you, the voman that he has given me."

"Jens . . . ?"

"Silence, voman! I have vone thing more to say, und then ve vill speak no more of this until ve are settled in Fort Ephraim."

Stunned, the woman could but listen in amazement as her husband continued.

"As you say, voman, ve may be in great danger from the Indians. I yust vant to tell you that I feel from prayer that at least some of us are safe und vill survive. I hope vith all my heart that ve all do, but I do not feel it. So I vant you to understand that should trouble come I vill do all in my power to protect you und our daughter. Even . . ."

Here the old man lost control of his voice for a moment, and the woman trembled as she felt the strength and power of his arms as he held her close to him as he had never done before. At length, when he was able, he continued.

"Even vill I protect you if it means that I must die to do so!"

"Jens, don't say that!" she cried.

"Now, voman," he said soothingly, "do not vorry. I have no fear of death, for I have the hope und the promise I spoke of before. I do not vant to be separated from the vones I love. Ja, that thought is hard to bear. But then . . . it is not so bad after all, for it is only for a little vile, und Kjersta und our son avait me there. Ve have that promise from the Lord, the promise of a resurrection und of living together eternally as husband und vife. That vas vy ve vere sealed. I know vith all my heart that that is true, und so my vorries are taken avay in the Lord.

"Now come und let us vake the others. It is time to be up und busy at getting the vagon repaired."

Jens Jergensen turned and strode toward the sleeping Terkelsen, leaving the woman standing silent and alone with her thoughts.

She was impressed. There was no doubt of that. But what did all this really change? Just because she might have been wrong about him did not eliminate the need she felt to escape the terrifying emotions, the need and love for others, that she felt sinking ever more deeply into her heart and soul.

No, she must leave her husband and his little daughter at the first opportunity, for never again would she accept the responsibility of love that Jens had spoken of. She admitted easily that she was being selfish, just as he said, but somehow that didn't seem so bad when placed beside the pain and horror she had experienced in the past because of her love. That must never happen again, and it was up to her to see that it wouldn't. Let him believe as he wished. It really didn't matter.

Besides, she thought, as she began to prepare breakfast, chances were that before long he too would learn firsthand how hard it was to really bear pain and grief. Then he and everyone else would know it was one thing to talk about bravely fighting and dying for a loved one, and quite another thing to actually do it.

Smiling, the woman felt confident that Jens Jergensen, her Jens Jergensen as he called himself, would fall far short of the mark he had so confidently set for himself. Yes, he would fall far short indeed.

Two things bothered her, though. When Kjersta and the baby had died, Jens had surely seemed able to handle that pain. Was she wrong? And another thing, how had Jens known of all those thoughts and feelings she had never expressed to another soul? In many ways she could not understand her husband. He seemed to have access to something that she surely didn't. Could it be possible . . . ?

CHAPTER NINE

The sun was just clearing the rolling hills to the east when Hoskoots reined in on the ridge above the encampment. Before going down he must settle his troubled and jittery nerves. Never must the People know of the fear and anxiety he felt.

He slipped from the back of his pony and allowed him to graze while he lay down in the shade of a gnarled old juniper. Wrapping his blanket around him against the morning chill he struggled with his thoughts for some time before finally dozing off. It was three hours before the sun, beating unmercifully on his recently exposed face, awakened him.

As he sat up and looked around Hoskoots marveled at the beauty of the day. No clouds darkened the azure sky, and above him in the juniper little birds were filling the air with song.

Hoskoots loved the birds. Many times he sat for hours listening to them and watching them. He considered them his little sisters. He longed to stay now and enjoy their company, for he dreaded going into camp. Peteetneet must know of all he had seen. But he did not fear Peteetneet. It was Tackwitch, the medicine man, whom Hoskoots feared.

The Ute encampment was not much to look at. A scattering of low brush-covered wickiups and here and there one covered with skin were all the nomadic Utes ever used for homes.

Naked children ran screaming here and there, and squaws of all sizes and ages were busily engaged in the work of the encampment, cooking and drying meat, tanning hides, gambling, and so on.

The Utes had no formal marriage ceremony that a white man would identify as such. Their system, highly practical for their society, was simple. If a man wanted a wife he bought her. Payment could be with horses or any other valuable item, but the system was designed to compensate the father or previous husband for the loss of labor force he experienced when the woman was gone. For, other than hunting and fighting, the women did all the work of the encampment.

When a man came in from a hunt, if he had been successful, the women unloaded the meat, unsaddled his horse, and then cooked and dried the meat. The man did nothing then until the meat was gone, when the squaw went out and got his pony, saddled it, and gave it to him. He then mounted and rode off to hunt again.

For the man it was a good life, and when Hoskoots rode into the camp the majority of the Ute warriors were scattered here and there, lazily gambling or racing their horses against each other along the nearby stream.

Hoskoots rode straight to the wickiup of Peteetneet, looking neither to the right nor to the left as he did so. Dismounting, he entered and squatted silently on the ground. After an appropriate silence the chief greeted him. Peteetneet had no great love for this ugly warrior who usually scorned the company of his band. Still, he must be polite as the man had come to visit him. For a little they smoked in silence the pipe that Peteetneet's old squaw had given them. As his eyes became used to the darkness Hoskoots became aware of a younger squaw sitting huddled back in the shadows nursing her child. There was a third wife, he knew, but she was not in the wickiup.

Finally Peteetneet gave the signal and Hoskoots had permission to speak. He did so, very carefully constructing his story so that as little bad light as possible was shed upon him. Hoskoots had no desire to appear a coward in front of his people.

When he had finished the old chief sat unmoving for some time, though Hoskoots could hear the excited whispering of the squaws behind him. At last, though, Peteetneet sent his oldest squaw for Tackwitch, the much feared and much respected old medicine man.

When at length the wise one, his wrinkled face reminding Hoskoots of sun-dried green hide, shuffled into the wickiup, the work of the old squaw was well done. The story of Hoskoots, glamorized as only a ghost story can be glamorized when told by those who believe in ghosts, was buzzing its way among the women throughout the whole camp.

To Tackwitch Hoskoots repeated essentially what he had told Peteetneet, though he was frequently interrupted by the chief as that worthy added details that quite surprised Hoskoots. He even wondered why he hadn't thought of those things.

There followed a long silence during which Hoskoots waited uneasily. He was afraid of old Tackwitch, as were most of the other Utes that he knew. Peteetneet was a powerful warrior, but Tackwitch was much more powerful than that. He could stand in the fire unharmed. Yes, but even more fearful than that was his ability to scratch the names of others on slips of paper.

Of course Hoskoots knew, as did all the other Utes, that if a name were ever scratched on paper then the man with that name was doomed. It was a fearful thing to watch that wrinkled old man scratching names on his tiny slips of paper. Worse than that, though, was the uncertainty they lived under from then on. Old Tackwitch, the wise one, was the only one who could read his medicine writing, and he would never reveal to the Utes the names he had scratched. At least he never would until a man was dead. Then he would strut forward waving his paper in the air, loudly proclaiming that it was as he had foretold, for was not the name of the dead man on his paper? To Hoskoots and the others it was a fearful thing indeed to see his great power. Thus was Hoskoots' fear of the wrinkled old man.

Suddenly the old medicine man stood and pointed to the door.

"Go now, Ugly One! I must think."

Hoskoots left immediately, though once outside he wondered where he should go or what he should do. These were his people, yet he really wasn't a part of them. Aimlessly he wandered, and in his mind was the hope that he might see Chipetz. Still, what good would it do to see her? He was still a poor man, he was still an ugly man, and he had no way of purchasing a wife.

From the wickiup of Peteetneet now came the low chanting and singing of old Tackwitch. Hoskoots was certain there was a great medicine coming.

Now Hoskoots became aware of another strange thing. People everywhere were staring and pointing at him. Then he realized that a dozen or so children were silently following him. Turning he shouted and waved his arms at them, and as a single person they fled screaming. Now Hoskoots was truly amazed. Always he had been taunted by the children, who seemed to take great delight in pelting him with small stones and sticks, always staying just out of reach. Now they fled from him in terror, and Hoskoots could not understand why. Next he noticed the maidens, the eligible females of the camp. As he approached they would smile or giggle and turn coyly away from him to busily engage themselves in whatever they were doing.

To be sure Hoskoots was pleased, but he was also puzzled. These maidens had never acted like this, not ever. Usually, if he was not ignored, these same females would taunt him about his face and occasionally even spit at him. That was one of the reasons he stayed away so much.

But suddenly all was changed, and he even wondered if perhaps his face had returned to the way it was before his accident. But no, his probing fingers told him that was not correct. Well, what was it, then, that made these people act as they were doing?

Before long Hoskoots spied Ankawakeets, a huge young warrior who was perhaps his closest acquaintance. Always before Ankawakeets had associated with Hoskoots only involuntarily, doing his best to be inconspicuous in the presence of this social outcast.

Now, though, as they saw each other, Ankawakeets yelled out and then strode over to the bewildered Hoskoots. Together they walked to a grassy spot near the stream where Ankawakeets demanded that Hoskoots tell him, his best friend, all about the white witch and the ghost camp where he had been held prisoner for so long. Furthermore the big Indian wanted to know all about the magic powers that Hoskoots was given by the spirits that enabled him to escape the terrible powers of his evil white spirit captors.

Hoskoots, beginning to realize that the old squaw had spread the story, was equal to the occasion. He told his story, but oh how it grew in the telling.

It was not long before Hoskoots and Ankawakeets were joined by Namowah and Tutsegavit, eager also to hear of this marvelous adventure. As the story unfolded the three listeners, flanked on all sides by silent staring children, grunted in admiration or shouted in alarm as they listened eagerly to the Ugly One.

In elaborate detail Hoskoots related to them each new crisis brought about by the spirit camp and the white witch who traveled with it. The red stallion grew too, assuming supernatural powers as it was held against its will by the evil spirits. But most marvelous of all to his listeners was the heroic way in which Hoskoots was able to gain control of every misfortune and bit of witchcraft the white woman had thrown his way.

It was by now a beautiful and fantastic story, one that would enhance the firesides of many a wickiup during the cold winter nights of years to come. By the time Hoskoots was finished telling it for the third time he had convinced even himself of its truthfulness and of his great power and wisdom. Yes, he, Hoskoots, was a mighty man indeed!

After the fifth telling, things settled down a little, and Hoskoots became aware again of the monotonous chanting of old Tackwitch. Would that old man never stop?

The four young warriors sat in the sultry shade together now doing nothing and thinking little more. In the midday heat the sounds of the camp died down, and only occasionally would they hear the shrieks of some squaw as she gambled with sticks for trinkets of one kind or another. It didn't seem to matter whether they won or lost, they all shrieked anyway.

Hoskoots wondered where Chipetz was. He had seen no sign of her, and he wondered then if she had heard how great a man he was. He wanted to go find her and speak with her, but it would be impolite to leave these his friends who had now chosen to associate with him.

So they sat, and occasionally they grumbled of the whites, not the spirits of Hoskoots but the real whites who were filling up their lands and driving away their game. And what about Arapene, their big chief, who the three friends of Hoskoots thought of as an old woman blinded by age and responsibility? According to them he was too soft and too weak to be chief, and only Hoskoots remained silent as they expressed that opinion.

Hoskoots knew Arapene, knew his power as a warrior and his vicious temper when angered. He had seen Arapene, when angered once by the refusal of some white Mormonees to buy a little child he had taken captive, take the child by the heels and dash his brains out on the ground. Hoskoots shuddered as he recalled the terrible temper of Arapene.

Hoskoots was content to let the man be chief, simply because it was easy that way to avoid him. This was especially true since Arapene had apparently changed his ways and was now spending so much time with Brigham Young and the other Mormonees.

To Hoskoots the biggest worry was old Tackwitch, the man of the dried leather face. He was the one to avoid. And until that day Hoskoots had been successful in doing just that.

Ankawakeets wanted to hear again of the red stallion spirit, and Hoskoots was only too happy to oblige, declaring unashamedly that the horse could fly through the air and also vanish at will. He was tethered by a magic tether or rope and only Hoskoots had the power to cut it and free the stallion. The spirits had destined that horse to be his.

The others grunted in admiration at this and wished that they too might be smiled upon by the spirits.

Perhaps the three of them had mistreated the Ugly One. Perhaps he only looked as he did so the spirits could recognize him. It was Namowah who suggested this, but Tutsegavit and Ankawakeets instantly saw the truth of it and agreed.

Hoskoots sat in stunned silence. What he was hearing was almost beyond belief, yet it should not be, for suddenly he too knew that Namowah had but spoken the truth. He was a favored son, and as he thought more of it his chest swelled in pride.

There was little chance though to bask in his latest glory, for at that moment there was a loud shriek and Peteetneet fled out of his wickiup, followed shortly by the wrinkled old Tackwitch.

Moving rapidly for one of his age he stalked toward Hoskoots, a strange fire flashing in his eyes. In alarm Hoskoots leaped to his feet while his three friends shrank a little behind him. They too feared this old man.

Tackwitch stopped in front of Hoskoots, glared into his eyes, then raised his bony old arms toward the sky.

"Hoskoots, the Great Spirit has shown me in vision the camp of which you speak. It is indeed, as you said, the camp of great and evil spirits.

"The stallion too is spirit, but it is good and is being held captive by the white witch. To you, Hoskoots, is given the power to free the horse. If you do you will be granted the power to destroy all the evil spirits of the camp. If you do not . . ."

Here the old man waved his hands in finality, and Hoskoots understood instantly what he meant.

"One thing more. If you set the stallion free and can mount him, then to you will be given the power to ride him in safety through battle of all sorts, even to the last day of your life. But all this must be done now, this day. You must go!"

A great fear rose up in the chest of Hoskoots. Vividly in his mind he could see the wicked gleam of the rifle in the hands of that witch-woman. He had no desire to return there, no desire at all. This was not what he had expected, and he wondered how he could have ever gotten into this predicament.

"I . . . I . . ."

"Wait!" Namowah shouted. "It is not right that the great Hoskoots should go alone. I myself request permission to go with him."

"I too!" shouted Ankawakeets.

"And I," added Tutsegavit, "if Hoskoots will allow it."

Hoskoots could not imagine that this was real. He was being asked to lead a war party against a camp of spirits. He was terrified. But, oh the glory and honor of it! With the help of these three men he could not fail. He must accept.

"There is much glory there," he spoke slowly. "I would be honored to have these three ride with me."

Tackwitch grunted and glared at them all. He then turned his back to them and whispered rapidly with Peteetneet. He then faced them again, grunting as he did so.

"It is a good choice. The four of you may go. Remember to heed the spirit of the red stallion. You see I have a paper here!"

There was an audible gasp from the whole assembly as Tackwitch held up a tiny slip of white paper covered with smudged marks.

"On this paper I have scratched the names of those who will die this day. Beware!"

"Women, bring these warriors their horses. They go now."

En masse every woman in the group fled to the horse herd, where four of the best horses, never mind who the owners were, were captured and brought forward. The four young men were then whooped out of camp.

And as they rode past the last wickiup Hoskoots looked back and saw Chipetz squatted in the doorway smiling demurely and waving at him.

Hoskoots was startled and pleased at the same time. Chipetz was a well-formed maiden of a surety. As he thought of her his heart beat faster and he longed with all his heart to return and enter into her wickiup.

Ah well, soon he would have that red stallion and then things would be different. By darkness he would have visited old Panguts, her father, and then . . . Weren't glory and honor wonderful things? See how much they had brought him already. Why, this would be the most memorable day of his life! And tonight, with Chipetz . . . Ah, if thoughts were only deeds.

The sun was sliding down the afternoon side of the heavens when the four Ute warriors rode out of camp accompanied by the boisterous well-wishes of the People, by the salute of old Tackwitch, and by a shadow that glided noiselessly along the hills above and behind them.

They rode with eagerness, they rode with anticipation, and they rode with death.

CHAPTER TEN

"Hei, Christian! Hurry up vith that vood, vill you? Ve must get this fire much hotter!"

"Oh for pete's sake keep your shirt on. I am hurrying," grumbled Christian. "Hey, Brother Terkelsen, gimme a hand up here, will ya? This dang hill's steeper than the price of rotgut whiskey in Salt Lake City. I can't hardly keep my feet on it. Come on up and help!"

"Christian, you vatch your tongue und you get that dang vood as you vas told. I am busy getting the vater. Brother Jergensen, how much of this vater do ve have to have?"

"Yust enough to cool the iron tire, Brother Terkelsen. Here, put that bucket over here out of the vay. Good. Voman, do you have the hole ready und the vheel on the ground all even?"

"Yes, Jens. As far as I can tell it is ready. How much longer do you think that fire will take?"

"Oh, yust a little. Ve yust have to get the iron tire red-hot und expanded. If Christian vould bring that vood more quickly it vould be ready much sooner. Hei, Christian! Vhere is that vood?"

"It's coming, it's coming! Just relax! This dang wood is heavier than a fat lady in a sideshow.

"Shoot," he grumbled. "That dang Jergensen's got no more patience than an old buffalo bull with bad wisdom teeth. Him and his dang Indians. I'll bet he never even saw one. Why, I'll bet him and that woman saw some shadow and it scared them. If there'd been any Indians around we'd have known it too. Me and old Terkelsen don't sleep that deep. Besides, why would a Ute warrior ever run from that girl?

"Gosh, this stuff is heavy! How in heck do they expect me to drag all this dang wood clear down to that supid fire? What I need is Terkelsen's horse.

"Say, I wonder if . . .

"Hey, Brother Terkelsen, if you ain't going to come and help, at least bring your horse up to me! This blasted wood's heavier than a forty-pound shot with no cannon to shoot it. How about it? Let me use your horse. All right?"

He was ignored this time, so again the young man began shouting.

"Brother Jergensen, tell Brother Terkelsen to lend me his horse! That way I can sure hurry more!"

The woman then looked up and spoke.

"Brother Terkelsen, you'd best lend that boy your horse. The way he's yelling up there he's liable to bring the whole Ute nation down on us. And like Christian would say, that'd be like a pack of wolves coming down on a fresh-born calf. You'd best lend that boy your horse."

Jens Terkelsen glared at the woman. She surely did have an uncomfortable way of putting things. And why in heaven's name was he taking orders from her? Or Brother Jergensen either, for that matter? What was going on around here?

"Ja," he grumbled, "und the vay you talk, voman, the Indians are here anyvay, so vat difference does it make?

"Young Christian, if you vant this horse you vill have to come und get it. I have lost nothing on that hill that vould make me vant to climb it. I am staying right here!"

"Yippee," shouted Christian as he scrambled down the hill to get the horse. "This is what I've been needing all along!"

The sun at last topped the hills and bathed the high ridges in early morning gold, and the woman caught her breath as she beheld the ethereal beauty of the sunbeams as they pierced the smoke slowly ascending from their large fire.

"Oh, Jens, aren't the mountains lovely in the morning? Look at how the dew sparkles on those aspen leaves up there in the sun. In a way I love it here. I wish we could stay and it would be like this always, with no problems and no worries. Don't you?"

Jens Jergensen, thinking of their earlier conversation, smiled and nodded in agreement. He was thrilled that his wife seemed happy, and he hoped that all was now well between them.

"Jens, look way up there on the mountain at those red cliffs. Wouldn't it be fun to be sitting up there on those cliffs with almost the whole world spread out below you? It would be like maybe God must feel, looking down on all this world of His."

Again Jens smiled. He was pleased, very pleased indeed, to hear his wife talking like this.

"Jens, how old do you think these mountains are?"

Startled a little at her question, and realizing that it was good for the woman to be talking, he turned to answer her.

"Vell, I vould say that they are very old, but then I guess not so old as other mountains."

"How can you tell that?"

"Vell, ve read in the scriptures that God created the earth in seven days, but I think the seven days spoken of are not the same as our days, but actually cover much longer periods of time."

"Why do you say that?"

"Yust because I have vatched, both here und in the old country, the earth around me, and vat I have seen leads me to believe that God vorks through natural laws in His dealings here, und He has spent much more time creating the earth than many of us are villing to admit.

"For instance, I think ven a mountain is new or young it has sharp or pointed ridges and peaks. As the mountain grows older the ridges vear down und the peaks vear off und the mountain becomes smooth und rounded. These mountains are fairly young because they are so sharp und pointed, but they are gradually being vorn avay by the vind, the rain, the snow, und so on. Ja, it does not happen quickly at all. If vat I see is correct there must be many more thousands of years involved here than the Bible vould seem to say.

"A seed vill fall into a crack, a plant vill grow, und the roots vill spread the crack a little vider. Then a rain vill come und the vater fills the crack, snow melts, und more vater goes in. Then it vill freeze, the vater vill expand like ve are trying to do vith the iron tire, und so does the crack expand. Eventually it vill chip avay und the rock vill roll down the hill breaking into smaller pieces as it rolls.

"Vind, snow, und vater vill continue to vork on it until after a very long time it vill be finally vorn down to soil vich vill fill in the low places of the mountains.

"The vater gathers in the low places too und becomes a stream. This vill flow down a mountainside becoming a brook und finally a river, always growing as more vater joins in. As the vater flows it vill tear out soil und rocks und drag them along vith it, gradually vearing them down into fine soil und sand vich is at last spread out into the valleys below, gradually building them up.

"The whole process goes on year after year in thousands of places und in thousands of vays.

"So a mountain vears down as it gets older, und thus the good Lord uses natural means vich He has set up, to build the earth und prepare it for the use of His children. God has spent a very long time preparing these valleys for our use, und now that ve are here ve vill reap the harvest of His labors und that is vy I say that all His vorks are for our ultimate good. Just as people vear down und get smoothed off during the years as their rough corners are knocked off by the rivers of life.

"Mountains, rivers, people, in a vay it is all the same thing. Ve are here, ve leave a few scratches on the good earth, und then ve are gone. Und who is left to know of our being here und of our going?

"Only those ve leave behind that treasure our memory. Und that is vy, my voman, that I say thanks to God every day for you und my little blue-eyed daughter."

The woman was speechless. How had he ever known all that? Why, the more she knew him the more she realized that she didn't know him at all. That didn't make much sense, but still . . .

"Voman, hand me more of the vood, vill you please? Ja, that is vat ve need. See how the iron tire is starting to glow?"

"Hey, Brother Jergensen, here's some more wood, lots more. Where do you want me to put it?"

"Yust right here, Christian. Yust right here. Ja, that fire is getting very varm. Hei, Brother Terkelsen! Come und help us throw on all this vood, und very soon the iron tire vill be hot enough to vork vith."

"Ja, Brother Jergensen, und then ve hurry und run, huh? Hah! If there really be Indians I tell you ve never outrun them vith that outfit. That is sure!"

"Ja, my brother, that is true. But I think my voman she scared them avay. I hope ve be troubled no more. Ja, I pray in my heart that it vill be so."

Christian looked carefully from one man to the other. He was tired of being the silent partner of this outfit. It was about time he spoke his piece. Why, he was full-growed. He surely ought to be entitled to a say. Mostly they kept him busier than a little dog in tall grass, but by thunder it was time he started speaking up!

"Well, Brother Jergensen, maybe she scared them away, and maybe she didn't. Maybe all that Indian ran for was to get a few of his friends. And maybe . . ."

Here he paused, wondering just how far he should go. They were all silent, giving him their full attention. A bell of caution clanged nervously in his mind, but recklessness being the way of all youth, young Christian Kjerulf plunged on.

"Maybe all either one of you saw was just some shadow. Maybe the both of you are just running scared, and there ain't no Indians at all."

Christian was never certain just how what happened next occurred, for he had no memory of Jens Jergensen moving at all. Besides, he was positive that the big Scandinavian was too old and too clumsy to do what he had just done.

All he could remember was that he had no more than finished speaking when there was a tremendous crash against his jaw, pinpoints of light pierced his brain, and then he was lying over by the wagon while Jens Jergensen knelt above him wiping his brow with a wet rag.

Oh how his jaw ached! Never had the young man been hit like that. He felt too old to suck and too young to die, but he was surely wishing he could do one or the other. He'd had no idea . . .

"Brother Kjerulf, I am sorry that I had to hit you. Ja, I am very very sorry. But I pretty dang near hit you again I vas so upset. You, of course, know that the voman does not lie, und neither do I!

"Ja, you must learn your manners again, young man, und I guess I must be the vone that vill teach you. If ve say that ve saw an Indian, then ve saw an Indian! If there vas doubt, ve vould say so. But Christian, even if ve vere mistaken und ve didn't see vone, ve both are still your elders. As such you must treat at least the voman vith respect. It is the only vay that a gentleman, a man, vill act. If you do not learn this important lesson, I promise you that your actions vill bring you only pain und sorrow.

"Now let me help you stand up und valk around a bit to steady your legs."

In a daze Christian struggled to his feet, and as his head slowly cleared all he could think about was this docile old man. He was amazed that Jens Jergensen could have taken care of him so quickly and effectively. And oh how his head hurt! He felt worse than a calf with the slobbers.

The woman too was surprised, and in a way she was, again, impressed. She felt only sorrow and pity for Christian, but then she had to admit that he had deserved what he got. But this man, her husband, well, the more she was with him the more she realized she didn't know him at all. He had always been so calm, so quiet. She would never have guessed that he had such a temper.

But no . . . that wasn't really the word either. He hadn't really lost his temper. He had merely reached out and with incredible swiftness drawn the young man to him where he lightly tapped the boy on the point of the chin with his fist. Then, before Christian could even slump to the ground Jens had lifted him in his arms and carried him to the wagon, where he began caring for him and bringing him back to consciousness.

The woman was amazed and from the look of shocked disbelief on Jens Terkelsen's face she knew that he had been as surprised as she was.

The woman had seen many fights and nearly as many men who called themselves fighters, and her father had taught her more than a little of their methods. But never had she seen a man act with such speed and such certainty of purpose as her husband had just done.

Even more incredible, though, was that now he was kneeling above the boy tenderly wiping his brow. The woman was stunned. But there was more. There were actually tears running down the face of her husband. She could hardly believe what she was seeing. Never had she known a man like him, nor had she ever guessed that there could be such a man. Certainly one did not expect to see tears in the eyes of a man, and she wondered if she felt ashamed to see them there.

But no, it wasn't shame. It was, well, more like a strange feeling of pride or joy or something akin to it, a feeling she could not recall ever experiencing before. In a way seeing Jens Jergensen crying because he had hurt Christian made her feel, well . . . it made her feel happy.

At that moment, more than ever before, the woman realized that despite herself she did feel love for this man who called himself her husband.

His fineness, his meekness, his gentleness *were* real. It was no show, no effort to impress others as she had mentally accused him of. Suddenly she was certain. Jens Jergensen was the genuine article, and no doubt of it, no doubt at all. Surely he had weaknesses, and yes he made many mistakes, but really, who didn't? That was just a part of life.

Now look at that! Jens was stoking the fire again, smiling at Christian and working with him as though nothing had happened. And

Christian was smiling back! It was incredible, yet it was so. How had Jens worked that?

Why had she never seen these qualities in him before? Why had this trip taken so long to come? Why must she learn of his goodness and his manliness when she had already taken the steps that would make it too late, forever too late, to return his love?

"Hei, Brother Terkelsen, how does the iron tire look to you?"

"Vell, it looks pretty dang good, but the fire is dying down."

"Ja? Vell then, yust put some more vood on it. I'll be vith you in a moment."

"Ja, ja," grumbled the old man called Jens Terkelsen. This business of taking orders was getting beyond the joke. Hadn't this move to Sanpete been his idea? And wasn't he the leader of this party? And if so then just why in the world was Jens Jergensen giving him orders?

Jens Terkelsen tossed another log onto the roaring fire and wondered at himself for doing it. Never before had he taken orders from anyone. Not ever! And yet here he was doing just what Jergensen told him to do without even an argument. Why, Jergensen was nothing more than a country blacksmith while he, Jens Terkelsen, was born to a far higher station in life.

Was he afraid of the other man? Maybe so, much as he hated to admit it. He surely had never seen a man move so quickly and so certainly as Jens Jergensen had just done against Christian. Somewhere in his memory, though, was something about his having once been a fighter, or been in some fights, or something like that. Exactly what he was trying to recall, however, evaded him. He shuddered then as he thought of a blow from those huge fists landing on his own jaw.

But there was more to it than that. It was, well . . . something undefinable. Something new in Jergensen's voice or actions spoke out suddenly of forceful power and leadership. As he thought about it he suddenly realized two things. He had never really been in command of this party, and in all the years he had known Jens Jergensen he had never really known him. It was strange how a man could go along for years feeling perfectly comfortable and have everything working just fine, and then suddenly he would turn a corner and look back and realize that he didn't even know where he'd been or what he'd been doing when he was there. It gave a man a funny feeling to realize that all this time he'd thought he was in charge of his own life it was in reality being directed by others. The thought made him feel like a puppet, and it angered him a little too.

He knew that from this point onward, whenever they were together in any sort of situation, he would never again be the leader of the two. It would just never work.

Jens Terkelsen was a good man. He was faithful to his religion, and Jens Jergensen considered him to be the best friend he had in the world. Yet as he considered these things something within him snapped, and he suddenly knew that at the first opportunity he would get away from this group. There were others who would appreciate his abilities more, and by rights he should be with them. He would watch, and when . . .

"Hei, brethren, the iron tire is glowing red-hot. Now is the time to put it on the vheel, und ve must all vork together.

"Voman, you stand over there by the vater, und be ready to pour fast ven I tell you.

"Christian, you und Brother Terkelsen use these sticks und prongs, und ve vill lift the iron tire out of the fire und then set it on the ground around the vheel."

"Are you all ready?

"Hei! Now ve all lift! Ah, good. Good."

"Jumping blue blazes, this thing is hotter than a burnt boot!"

"Ja, Christian, that it is. That it is. Ah, very good, by golly. Now ve ease it down carefully around the fellies of the vheel . . . good, good . . . Ooops! Brother Terkelsen, up a little! Quick! Now put that stick under it to hold it. Ja . . . that is right. Good."

"Voman, are you ready vith the vater?"

"I surely am. Just tell me when and where."

"Christian, is the iron tire even vith the vheel on your side?"

"Sure as new-platted rope is. But hey! The fellies are starting to smoke!"

"Ja, they vill a little. Brother Terkelsen?"

"Ja, my side is even."

"Now, voman, the vater! Quickly! Before the hot iron tire burns the fellies! Good. Good. Now, voman, ve all can help you. Brethren, ve must get as much vater as ve can on that vheel, und quickly too."

Great clouds of steam arose as the cool spring water splashed over the red-hot iron tire. Quickly it cooled and as it did so it contracted tightly around the fellies of the wheel, binding them together and holding them tightly against the spokes and the hub.

The wheel was fixed.

Within another half hour Jens Jergensen had the wheel mounted back on the wagon, the woman and Jens Terkelsen had the oxen yoked and chained, the fire was doused, and they were ready to roll.

Things seemed to be looking up. They surely did.

CHAPTER ELEVEN

The morning was late, but there was still a cool fresh wind coming down through the spruce, the aspen, and the pine trees. The wind had the smell of pines on its breath, the sound of aspen leaves dancing, and they could hear the sounds of cool water dancing over stones as the crystal liquid from the spring gurgled along down into Salt Creek.

A dim animal trail led down off the bench through the aspen and the cottonwood, and almost without thinking the man called Jens Jergensen geed the oxen down the faint path and braked the wagon into the creek bottom.

The woman sat high on the wagon seat with the baby girl held tightly in her arms, and she felt good. The crawly feeling so often on her neck of late was gone, and the world seemed just a little more secure to her.

Jens Terkelsen followed astride his big red stallion and Christian E. Kjerulf brought up the rear, hazing the cattle and goats before him and feeling contented that they were once again on their way to Sanpete.

The date was June 4, 1858.

Throughout the morning the oxen plodded slowly forward. Three times they had to cross Salt Creek, and except for the slippery stones on the bottom, the cool water was a relief from the dusty brush-choked bottomland trail.

At last the stream swung off to the northeast, and for a few moments they halted to gaze in wonder at the sand cliffs strung out in a gigantic amphitheater to the north of them where they ate into the rim of the hills above Salt Creek.

The party nooned on the eastern bank of Salt Creek and Jens Jergensen, after a short walk, commented on what a fine farm the rich bottomland would make. Perhaps he would one day come back and homestead it.

Christian grinned at the prospects. It might be a good place for Brother Jergensen, but it sure as blue blazes wasn't a good place for him! It was far too isolated. Anybody living here would be lonelier than an orphaned polecat. He wanted to be where people were. That was where a man could find real opportunity. Opportunity and girls. They were worth considering too. Still, after that incident earlier he surely respected Brother Jergensen's opinion.

Following lunch and a rest for the oxen the party started again up the canyon. The terrain was gradually changing, becoming less steep but more arid and barren on the hills.

The afternoon air was sticky now and still, and the dust they churned up hung in great choking clouds over the little band of pioneers, sifting over, around, and through everything and settling as a white layer of dust that soon turned to grimy mud on the sweaty bodies of the animals and people.

They came at last to Hop Creek, a little tributary that swirled through the bottoms to eventually join Salt Creek. Despite its small size the crossing was steep and proved to be immensely difficult.

Jens Jergensen sent the woman on ahead to wade the stream while he and the others carefully took the wagon across.

The woman waded over and then laid the baby down while she stooped and took a long drink of the cold fresh water.

She was like that, hand cupped to her mouth and enjoying the cold wetness of the stream, when the hair on her neck stood out and the old familiar horrors started crawling along her spine.

Slowly she dropped her hands and turning she scooped up her little daughter. Her eyes searched the skyline and the hills beneath but she could see nothing, nothing but a big old buzzard circling slowly in the still air above the canyon. Yet the woman knew someone was there, and cold terror gripped her heart.

Jens Jergensen, as he waded the small stream, glanced at his wife, and instinctively knew what was wrong.

"Voman, come here a moment."

"Jens?"

"Voman, have you seen something?"

"No . . . not really, but they're out there, and they are close. Jens, what are we going to do?"

"Voman, you are certain then?"

"Yes, yes, I'm certain!"

Without another word he turned back to the wagon and guided it up out of the stream bed. Then he turned back and walked to his wife.

"Voman, you get into the vagon vith the baby, und then you draw the cover closed tightly.

"Christian! Brother Terkelsen! Come quickly. I must speak vith you!"

"What's up?" asked Christian as he splashed across the stream ahead of the cattle.

"My brothers, ve have the Indians vith us again."

"Vell, vere are they then?" queried Jens Terkelsen, scorn and derision in his voice.

"They are here, Brother Terkelsen. They are here. Ve vill see them soon enough, I think. Now ve must decide vat ve vill do about it. Do you have any suggestions?"

"How about forting up?"

"I thought of that, Christian. Und ve could do it, too. But vith vat could ve defend our position if ve vere attacked? Then too, that might indicate that ve vere afraid of them."

"Vell, now is the time ven ve need those guns I vas trying to get you to buy. Don't say I didn't tell you so."

"Ja, Brother Terkelsen, you surely did. Und I am the first to admit that I have made a mistake. Still, ve don't know that they are hostile. Guns are only good for killing, und I vould rather not kill my red brothers. Vithout guns I feel there is much less possibility of a battle."

"Ja by golly," snorted Terkelsen. "There vould be no battle all right. Yust a massacre is all."

"Any other suggestions?"

"Yeh, I have another one. Let's all run like blue blazes."

"Und how vill you run, young man?" Jens Terkelsen grinned, and then continued. "You are afoot und they vill no doubt have horses. Can you run faster than a horse?"

"Well, there's yours. I expect it could be used."

"Vat do you mean?"

"Brother Terkelsen, sometimes you're slower than the eighth scab on the seven-year itch. I mean to put the woman, the child, and Brother Jergensen on your horse and give them a chance to get away. You and I, we ain't got no family, and maybe if they attacked we could hold them off for a little while."

"Ja, und vith vat? Ve already decided that ve have no guns."

"True, but I reckon we could fight with knives, or that pitchfork there, or anything else for that matter. All we'd have to do would be to slow them down."

"Ha," snorted Terkelsen.

"Now, brethren, there is no use in this fighting vith ourselves. Brother Terkelsen, you may keep your horse. Use it if you have to. The voman und me, ve vill stay vith you. Perhaps these Indians von't fight. Ve are at peace vith them, you remember. Perhaps it is only food that they vant. If so ve vill give them vat ve have und then ve all vill be happy."

"Yeh, but Brother Jergensen, what if they want more than food? Like the wagon or our cattle or something?"

"Vell, then ve give them the vagon, und vile they are taking it maybe ve can show them that ve mean vat ve say about brotherly love. Vasn't it Jesus who said that if a man asked me to go vith him a mile then I must go vith him two? Und didn't He also say that if a man vanted my coat I must give him my cloak also? Vell, He vas teaching us to really care for others, und vat kind of a Mormon vould I be if I didn't do vat Jesus said?"

"All of that sounds very noble, my friend Brother Jergensen. If you really mean it then you are a good man. But tell me, vat if that same Indian vanted very badly your vife und your little daughter? Und he also vanted you dead. Vat vould you do then, my noble friend?"

All were silent then as they thought of what none of them wanted to consider. Into each mind came the memory of the stories of murdered Mormons told the night before, and these four all knew what an Indian would do to the woman if one ever captured her. None of them wanted to think of it, but it was there before them to be considered.

The afternoon sun beat upon them as they stood in silence. Even the noisy ripple of the small stream seemed muted. The oxen, cattle, and even the goats stood still in the sultry heat, and the silence was oppressive.

Christian, unable to bear the tension any longer, and feeling sorry for old Brother Jergensen, made an effort to ease it.

"My gosh, it's hotter than a fried mustard plaster here in the sun. If we had any chickens, they'd be laying hard-boiled eggs. Come on, let's hit the shade."

No one moved, and there was no response to his remark. A little irritated, he spoke again.

"Will somebody say something? It's so dang quiet a man could hear a cricket sigh. At least he could if they hadn't all been fried in this heat." When no one responded even to this, he belatedly realized that it was not then a proper time for humor.

At last the red stallion snorted, and when he did so Jens Jergensen raised his head and looked into the wagon at his wife and daughter.

For a long time their eyes held in unspoken communication, and then at last he spoke.

"There comes a time, according to the Lord, ven a man must stand up and fight for vat is his.

"In the Book of Mormon, in chapter 48 of Alma, ve are told that the Nephites vere commanded to fight in defense of their lives und the lives of their loved vones, even to the shedding of blood. Ja, but they vere never to give offense, but vere to show love und respect venever it vas possible.

"No man who is a true man vants to fight, for he knows that all men are brothers. But in defense of right a man sometimes is called upon to do that vich he does not choose.

"There vas a time, not too long ago, ven the voman und I vere married by vone who held the priesthood of God. Und ven that brother married us he spoke of a scripture in Matthew. There Jesus said that ven a man married a voman they vere to be no more twain but vone flesh. Then the Lord said, 'Vat therefore God hath joined together, let no man put asunder.'

"My friend Brother Terkelsen, if an Indian or anyvone else should try to put this voman whom I love, und I, asunder, then I vould do my best to stop him. I surely vould. But I vould try to be peaceful first, as I have said all along!"

"Well then, let's get going," shouted Christian. "If we hurry, then maybe no one will try."

"Vone moment, Christian. Before ve go on I think it vould be a great help to all of us if ve pray again. I know ve did this morning, but I vould like to pray now. Vill you join me?"

If the Utes were watching the little group it must have appeared strange to see the three men slowly drop to their knees in the dust and rocks of Salt Creek Canyon. Even the woman in the wagon, the one who had professed to disbelieve their faith, fell to her knees on the wagon box floor while she listened with rapt attention to the softly speaking voice of her husband. His words were simple and yet nervously direct, and the thought came to the woman that this man prayed as though he knew intimately the one he was speaking with.

"Dear Father, there may be little time for us to pray, but ve yust vanted to stop und say thank you for all our blessings. God, these mountains are surely beautiful, und ve are happy that ve have been able to travel through them in this land of Zion. Now there be those here, the Lamanites, who live in these beautiful mountains. Today ve especially pray for them. Help us please to love them und to teach them more of thee.

"Now if ve can, ve vould like to travel on in peace to Fort Ephraim. But God, if ve must fight, then bless us that ve may do so without malice or hatred. For ve know these Lamanites do not understand the Gospel as ve do.

"If ve have done wrong, please forgive us. Und especially help us to always try to do better. In Jesus' name ve pray, Amen."

The woman, moved to tears, looked out of the wagon at her husband, and she found him watching her, a calm smile upon his face.

Slowly then Jens Jergensen arose and faced the others.

"Brethren, I yust vant you to know how much I care for each of you. My voman und I vill be eternally thankful for your friendship. May God bless you both.

"Now as Christian yust said, it is hotter here than a fried mustard plaster, vatever that is. Vat you say ve be on our vay to Uinta Springs?"

Slowly then the wagon rolled eastward through the canyon. Christian found that there was no need to shout at the animals, for they seemed intimidated by the oppressive silence and willing to move as he guided them. He felt it too, and he was certain the others did.

The woman, baking in the oven-hot interior of the closed wagon, watched her husband through a crack in the canvas. Strangely enough she felt calm, and she was certain, probably because Jens was, that whatever happened would be for the best. She peered through the crack again and wondered, no, worried over in her mind the same question she had been stewing around with all morning. Why, oh why, had it taken until now to learn what Jens Jergensen was really like? If she had only known, what a difference it might have made.

They had traveled scarcely a mile from Hop Creek when the Utes swooped down on them out of a draw to the north, and the attack came so swiftly and with such violence that even though each of the pioneers had prepared himself for such an event, each was still caught totally by surprise.

In the first volley fired by the Utes a ball slammed into the saddle horn of the red stallion and Jens Terkelsen was thrown, badly frightened, to the ground.

At almost that same instant young Christian E. Kjerulf was knocked sprawling with an arrow in his back.

But the first death was not that of a white man. As the Utes under Hoskoots spewed out of the mouth of the draw a shadow drifted down the hill to the point they were passing. None of them saw it, but why should they have? It was a shadow, nothing more.

Yet from that shadow sped an arrow which slammed into the back of Namowah, and without a sound he slid from the back of his running horse and fell to the ground. But he felt no pain, for he was dead. And the others rode on, unaware of his passing, or of the presence of Inepegut, the crazy Killer.

The Salt Creek Canyon Massacre had begun.

CHAPTER TWELVE

Dazed and shaken, Jens Terkelsen pushed himself off the ground. His head reeled with pain from where he had struck it in his fall, and for a moment he wasn't certain just what had happened. He looked around for his horse and finally saw it buckjumping up the canyon, an Indian racing after it.

An Indian!

They were under attack! The woman had been right all along! It was only then that he realized the significance of the awful din that had been assaulting his ears. It was the screaming and screeching of a war party of Utes.

They were in grave danger.

He was in grave danger!

Hastily he turned to look at the wagon, and the first thing he saw was young Christian lying on the ground with an arrow in his back. Then into his still blurry vision flooded the Indians, whooping past him toward the wagon.

Jens Terkelsen was not a man to spend all day making snap decisions, and he wasted no time now. The Utes were after the wagon and so for the moment, as far as he could tell, he was unobserved. There was nothing he could do to help Brother Jergensen and the woman, and Christian was beyond help. Therefore he could best help all by escaping himself.

Suiting thought to action he lunged across the gravel flat and slid into a small ravine. Here he paused for an instant to determine if he was followed, and then he broke into a stopping run down the ravine.

It was perhaps thirty yards from where he entered the arroyo to the steep hills on the south of the canyon, and he reached them in seconds. Scrambling carefully now in order to make as little noise as possible Jens Terkelsen crawled up through the thick stands of oak that choked the low hills.

His breath was coming now in ragged gasps, his leg hurt, and he was terrified at the noise he made as he crawled through the thick layer of old dead leaves.

Yet he dared not stop! He was still too close to the wagon and to those hideously awful Indians. Jergensen and his brotherly love! Humph! Only an idiot could love those creatures. How was Jergensen loving the Indians now, he wondered, almost grinning at the thought, and then feeling guilty because of it.

At last he reached the brow of the low hill, and there before him loomed the giant bulwarks of the high mountains.

He was exhausted! There was no way he could go any farther. At least not until he'd had a few moments' rest.

Quickly he looked around. He had to have cover, somewhere to hide at least until he got his wind back.

Besides, there was something wrong with his leg. He wanted to look at it, to see what was wrong, but there was no time. First he had to find cover.

There, on the other side of that clearing! That old deadfall with the rocks around it looked as though it would be a good place to hide. It was a little higher than anywhere else around, and from there he could at least see what was approaching him.

Still doubled over he zigzagged across the clearing, bearing to the left of where he was actually going. Then, just at the last moment, he veered over and leaped headlong into the space beyond the rocks, where he rolled to a stop beneath the old deadfall.

Perfect!

Now he must remain still until he could move on.

Slowly his breathing returned to normal, and he began to take stock of his situation. He was well hidden and at least two hundred yards from the wagon. He was also unarmed! No, no, he wasn't. He had his knife. Jens Terkelsen had never used a knife to fight with, but he was certain that he could if he should need to.

There was that pain in his leg again, the leg that hadn't worked properly as he was climbing up the hill.

Carefully he looked down, and to his surprise and dismay he saw a jagged gash in the flesy part of his thigh.

He was wounded!

The bullet that had hit his saddle, of course! It must have ricocheted up through his leg. For a moment he felt sick, but then he got ahold of himself and leaned over to examine the wound.

Fortunately it was not deep, and it looked a lot worse than it really was. Tearing a strip of cloth from his shirt Jens Terkelsen bound it around his leg. Then he lay back again.

He was still in a good position. Carefully he examined everything around him. All was as it should be. It was quiet. Maybe it was too quiet. He had heard others talk of that, but how could they tell? Quiet was quiet. So far as he could tell he was alone in all the world.

Overhead a small cloud drifted across the face of the blue sky, and the warmth of the sun, slowly seeping into his aching body, made him feel oh so sleepy.

It was very quiet! Only occasionally did the faint sound of yelling and screaming drift up over the brow of the hill and into his pounding ears.

That was surely too bad about those folks down there. He wished there was something he could have done. Why, they should have run as he did. It might have been hard for the woman, carrying the baby as she would have had to do, but still it could be done. In a situation like that it was every man for himself, every woman for herself!

And look at him. He was safe now. Because of a wise snap decision he was safe. In an hour or so he would leave here and walk back to Nephi. Yes, and eventually he would still be a power to reckon with in Sanpete Valley.

Ah, the world was looking good to Jens Terkelsen.

Very, very good!

When Jens Jergensen first heard the shouts of the Indians and the pounding hoofbeats of their horses he was walking along on the side of the wagon opposite where they were.

A rifle ball ripped through the canvas of the wagon above his head and he instinctively ducked. Then as realization came he leaped for the front of the wagon, shouting as he ran.

"Voman, get the baby und lay down! If the vagon stops then you get out und run, und don't you stop!"

"What about you?" she screamed.

"I vill hold them if I can, und then I vill be along. Do not vorry. All vill be vell!"

Jens Jergensen shouted and slapped at the oxen until they finally broke into a lumbering run. However, this lasted for not more than five or six yards before they stopped altogether.

There was no time to push them further, so he grabbed the pitch-fork from the side of the wagon where it was secured behind the water barrel and turned to face the Utes.

It was only a split second before the Indians were upon him, but the mind of Jens Jergensen moved with amazing rapidity and clarity.

He saw the red stallion being pursued up the canyon by one of the Utes, and then he saw Christian Kjerulf lying on his face just a few yards off with an arrow protruding from his back.

"Not Christian," he thought. "He is much too young for this."

A movement far to the side caught his attention and he distinctly saw Jens Terkelsen slide into a ravine and disappear from sight.

Immediately he was pleased that his old friend had escaped, and so he turned his attention to matters more pressing to himself.

He thought then of his promise to the others that he would try to make peace before he fought, and he realized that these Utes had taken that decision out of his hands. Well, so be it. He would have tried if he could.

In all the dust it was hard to see with any degree of certainty, but it looked as if there were only three Indians coming toward him.

No . . . wait a moment! There were three horses, but it looked as if only two of them were mounted.

Only two?

Then where would all the others be? Surely the Utes would not attack with such a small force. It made no kind of sense, no kind of sense at all. Maybe . . .

He heard a swish and felt something tug at his shoulder. An arrow! That man in the rear, the big one . . .

And then the Indians were upon him.

Jens Jergensen stood, feet wide apart, and swung the pitchfork like a giant club, and the Indian closest to him, the one swinging the hatchet, vanished from his sight.

But there was no time to think, to wonder, to consider what was happening, for he felt the heavy shock of something tearing at his chest, heard a deafening explosion, and then he was knocked rolling.

His next realization was that the heavy body of a Ute warrior was crushing him to the ground and then the man called Jens Jergensen saw something flash in the Indian's upraised hand.

A knife!

Almost blindly he reached up to stop the thrust of the blade, and as he did so he yelled again at the top of his lungs.

"Voman, take our daughter und run! You must save our daughter . . . Go now! Quickly! Vile I . . ."

The woman in the wagon lay transfixed. She simply could not move. Through the rear of the wagon she could see the entire battle scene, and each detail burned itself permanently into her mind.

She saw her husband, the man she had never before this day appreciated, knock an Indian from his horse with a pitchfork. Then, before he could get set again she saw him hunch his shoulders a little as if from some unseen blow. Then the other Indian hit him and they both went sprawling into the dust and dirt of Salt Creek Canyon.

There was a knife! That Indian had a knife, and he was on top!

"Jens! Jens!"

He was yelling at her now, telling her to run, to take the baby and run. But how could she leave? How could he possibly expect her to run off and leave him? She never could do that. Not now, not after the things she had experienced today.

Where . . . oh where was Brother Terkelsen? Or Christian? Why didn't they come and help? How could she help him? There must be some way . . .

"Jens!" she screamed. "Your knife! Get out your knife! Oh, my little daughter," she sobbed. "What are we to do? How can I help your papa? God, please help my husband . . ."

The world was a spinning blackness to Christian E. Kjerulf. White and yellow lights were spiraling through that blackness. On and on and on and on.

It seemed so peaceful, but somewhere there was a terrible noise. It was screaming! It was a woman screaming!

But why? Why was she screaming? He wished she'd stop. He so wanted to just lie there and enjoy the darkness and the quietness . . .

Why did his back and shoulder hurt so badly? And his chest hurt too. It hurt awfully just breathing. Why hadn't he noticed that before?

What was wrong? He had to get up, to see!

Struggling up a little he forced himself to open his eyes, and as they spun slowly into focus he saw the Indians, one lying on the ground near him with a great red gash along the side of his head, and the other struggling atop Brother Jergensen.

Christian had to help! He had to get over there and help Brother Jergensen.

Christian Kjerulf pushed himself up farther and as he did so he saw something else. There was blood on the ground beneath him.

His blood!

He was spitting blood!

Why would he be spitting blood? And what was that thing sticking out through his shirt? It looked like an arrowhead, an Indian arrowhead.

It couldn't be!

But no matter whether it was or not, he had to get to Brother Jergensen. He needed his help . . . But it was so dark again. He had to get . . . to get . . . Where had they all gone? How could he find them when it was so dark? How . . . ?

CHAPTER THIRTEEN

High on the hill under an old deadfall the man called Jens Terkelsen yawned and shifted his position. He was surely sleepy. It was good to feel safe again.

Maybe he could take a short nap before he moved on. His knife was close should he need it, but he was certain he wouldn't. Not now.

One more look and he would relax a little. Maybe even sleep. There was surely . . .

Suddenly his breath caught. What was that?

WHAT WAS THAT NOISE?

With his breath held still he strained to hear, to determine if the small sound he had heard, of something whispering quickly over something else, would come again.

With a feeling approaching terror he peered over the rocks and the dead tree, gazing all about. Something, something or somebody, was near, was coming toward him!

But there was nothing . . .

Really worried now he got to his feet to check the area again. But nothing had changed, nothing at all. As far as he could tell the oak and pine, the sparse grass, even the rocks were exactly as they had been a few moments before.

It was awfully quiet. Even the air was still.

For some reason he felt he should move on, his gut feeling was to move on quickly. Yet his reason told him that this place was a good one to hide in, and that he should remain in it until he had rested. Still, if something was that close to him . . . ?

But nothing was there. Nothing at all.

Jens Terkelsen dropped back to the ground again, certain that he was as alone as he had ever been. His leg hurt, and he reached back to shift himself into a more comfortable position. And when he did so a muscular arm slid from out of nowhere and encircled his throat, jerking him violently back and shutting his breath off.

For an instant he was so surprised that he could not react, but then instinct took over and he began fighting with his hands, trying to tear the arm from his neck, trying to get his breath back again. Now pressure was building in his head, a pressure that made his eyes feel as though they were going to burst. Suddenly there were lights popping, tiny pinpoints of light that kept bursting into blossoms of pain within his mind, blossoms of pain that increased the pressure until he was certain he could endure it no longer.

And that was when he realized that he was dying, that he was being murdered. His thoughts dashed rapidly then, to the time when he saved his younger sister from drowning, to the girl that he almost married, to his best friend Jens Jergensen, to the red horse that he had been so proud of, to his best friend Jens Jergensen . . . Why, he wondered, had he abandoned his best friend? If he could only do it over . . If only . . .

Slowly his body relaxed and his idea of land and power in Sanpete Valley was gone, his memories were gone, and then life was gone. In that hard old body so filled with determination and plans there was nothing, nothing at all.

The rifle ball that had slammed into Jens Terkelsen's saddle and then ricocheted off had frightened the red stallion terribly, but Hoskoots didn't know that.

He had fired the shot, his only shot that day, and he hadn't had time to reload his musket. Still, he was certain that he had killed the old man who was riding the stallion. He had fallen as though he were dead, and that bothered the Ute. Was it that easy to kill a spirit?

But now the horse wouldn't stop. Each time Hoskoots drew near the animal, off it would go again. It was maddening, and Hoskoots the Ugly One, man of little patience, was growing angry indeed. Already he was far beyond the sounds of battle, and that bothered him too. His friends might need his magic.

Still, he knew much of the three he had left there, Namowah, Tutsegavit and Ankawakeets.

Especially Ankawakeets!

He was a big man, a very big man. Hoskoots had never seen him defeated in any kind of battle, fun or otherwise.

No, he had no fears for his three companions. His only fear was that he might not catch the red stallion, this spirit horse that he must have.

Hadn't Tackwitch told him that once he was upon that horse he would be safe in battle for the rest of his life? Surely that was worth the effort.

He must catch the stallion! Now . . . if it would just stand still . . .

Jens Jergensen realized that he was about to be scalped. The knife was in the air and the Indian, his face streaked with paint and sweat, was grinning in anticipation.

Desperately he yanked his arm from beneath the Ute's knee and caught hold of the descending wrist, locking his elbow as he did so.

Ankawakeets grunted in surprise. He had shot this man in the chest, could even see the wound, and by all rights he should be dead. There should be no fight left here. Yet this man had pulled his arm free from under the Ute's knee as if it took no effort at all. This man could be a warrior . . .

The Ute was very strong, perhaps the strongest man Jens Jergensen had ever fought. He had to get him off. Somehow he had to throw the Indian off so he could get out his own knife, which was pinned beneath him.

The Indian was slippery, and he had the strangest odor about his body. Like oil and smoke and sage and he couldn't tell what else . . .

The woman was yelling at him. Why wasn't she running as he had told her to do? She had to get away! He must make certain that she and the baby escaped! He must get up . . . get up and make certain of her safety.

Suddenly he gave a mighty lunge and his other hand broke free. It was only for an instant, but that was enough. Twisting slightly he slammed up with his open palm catching the Ute's chin in his hand and snapping his head back. Heaving then he rolled and threw the dazed Indian to the side and then the man called Jens Jergensen struggled to his feet.

For a moment he stood, swaying drunkenly, trying to clear his head. For some reason it kept getting darker, and he was having trouble seeing. That pain in his chest . . . He had been hurt, he knew that much, but how badly?

He didn't dare look! Not now! The Ute was on his feet too, and he was holding his knife low, circling.

Desperately Jens Jergensen tried to clear his vision. For a moment things got very bright and he thought he was in a different place . . . The Ute! Forcing thoughts of all else from his mind he concentrated on the big Indian crouching before him. This was like old times . . .

The Ute suddenly charged, his blade flashing in the sunlight, and Jergensen sidestepped, feeling his homespun trousers part where the knife slashed them. That was close, but not as close as it could, no— should have been. And suddenly Jens Jergensen felt a burst of confidence. He could beat this man . . . For the woman and the child he would . . .

The Indian struck again and they both rolled into the dust, the Ute stabbing with his blade while Jergensen did his best to fend off the blows. Suddenly the old Mormon threw the Ute off, leaped to his feet, and with a roar of pain and anger, charged. Ankawakeets, surprised, stepped back, tripped, and they both fell into the brush, where they rolled apart.

The woman in the wagon lay as if transfixed by the scene before her. In horror she watched the knife of the Indian darting with snakelike rapidity at her husband, and she suddenly realized that she had never seen a more courageous man than Jens Jergensen. Why had she not seen that before? Why . . . ?

The two men circled each other warily, and the Ute suddenly thrust with his knife—another spot of blood appeared on Jergensen, high on his shoulder. The Ute was amazingly quick and agile for a man so large.

And his face—still, impassive, even hard. Not even in his eyes could the Mormon see emotion. Yet the Ute was feeling emotion, for he too was amazed! Never had he fought a man like this one.

Jens Jergensen, still unarmed, feigned a slip, and instantly the Indian sprang in, only to take the full force of the Mormon immigrant's right fist to his cheek and jaw.

Stunned and angered he sprang from the rocks where he had sprawled and swung his knife viciously, intent upon Jergensen's abdomen, his swing intended to disembowel. Jergensen had no choice but to take the blade in his arm, ignore the searing pain, and then lunge back. His huge fist slammed into the Indian's side, but the Ute swung around, striking swiftly again with his knife.

The blade went into Jergensen, but he steeled his mind against the additional pain, struck again powerfully with his fist, and then they both fell, rolling apart in the rocks. The Ute, twisting swiftly, sprang at him and Jens Jergensen rolled over and came up, struggling for breath. The Indian lunged to get close and Jergensen sidestepped, kicked swiftly, and tripped the Ute, who fell heavily into a clump of sage. When the Indian came up he had no knife.

They stood still now, staring at each other, and Jens Jergensen gulped in great tearing breaths of air to soothe his tortured lungs. Oh how his chest hurt! And there was the taste of blood in his mouth. His lungs must have been hit.

With a detached feeling he wondered if he might talk peace now with this Ute. He was the most marvelous fighter the man Jens Jergensen had ever come across. He would be honored to call this man his brother. Maybe if . . .

It was growing brighter again, and he seemed to be in another place. The hills were there, but somehow they were different, more green, more . . .

Slowly the Ute began to circle and Jens Jergensen, forcing himself to concentrate, circled with him. Each placed his feet with care and warily watched the other, for both understood now that at least one of them, and perhaps both, would die.

It would be finished here.

Suddenly the Ute seemed himself to stumble, and when he came again to his feet Jergensen caught the wicked gleam of the knife in his hand.

The Indian gripped the weapon more tightly and moved carefully toward the Scandinavian, sure that he could destroy him but unsure of what his cost would be. He had never guessed that such a man might be found among the whites.

All was still save for their heavy breathing. That and the voices. Jens Jergensen could hear people talking.

People talking?

The Scandinavian's mouth was dry and he clenched and unclenched his fists, warily circling his opponent.

The heat now seemed oppressive. Sweat began to trickle into Jergensen's cuts, causing them to burn and sting. His lips tasted salt from the sweat on his face. Salt and blood. And there were those voices again, strangely familiar and clear and yet sounding so far away.

Jens Jergensen started to move forward and the Ute feinted, then lunged quickly forward. Unable to knock the knife blow aside Jergensen struck it down, catching the Ute's arm in his hard old hand.

Closing his powerful fingers on the man's wrist he dug in, seeking the nerve there, to find it and paralyze the Ute's hand.

For a moment then they fought face to face, each straining against the other, the Ute trying to draw his knife up while Jergensen fought to hold it down.

Suddenly Jergensen slipped to the side, throwing Ankawakeets off balance, and before the Ute could set himself again the old Mormon smashed a hook to his face, and then, quickly, another.

Again they strained against each other, their bodies greasy with sweat and blood, and suddenly Jergensen found the nerve he was seeking, the median nerve in the Ute's wrist, and he began grinding upon it.

The Ute cried out and tried to back away, but Jergensen moved with him, not allowing the Indian an inch of free space, forcing him to step back to keep from falling, and no matter how desperately the Ute struggled the man Jens Jergensen stayed with him.

Suddenly the Indian cried out again and, opening his hand, let go of the knife.

Jens Jergensen then slugged the Ute, a short wicked blow to the body, and as they struggled together the Ute's fingers began creeping toward Jergensen's throat.

Desperately the big Scandinavian strained his head back, flexing his enormous arm and chest muscles hard against the Ute in an effort to pin his arms, to prevent his eager fingers from closing off his breath.

Desperately then they struggled, the one for his own life and the other for the lives of his family, and each at last understood the strength of his opponent.

Then suddenly they both fell to the ground and rolled over and over, and Jergensen's hold seemed to slip on the Indian. Instantly the Ute twisted to jump up, and then Jergensen's arms locked in a vice-like grip around the Ute's chest and he began to squeeze.

Harder and harder he squeezed, and the pressure on the Indian became unbearable. He tried to scream but couldn't, he flailed his arms and legs wildly in an effort to break loose, his face went bloodless, and he struggled desperately to relieve the pressure.

Jergensen, his face set and his eyes closed, rose slowly to his feet like a great angry wounded bear. The Ute struggled vainly in his arms, his back bent almost double by the pressure.

And then suddenly his spine snapped.

The Indian, Ankawakeets, at last cried out, his face reflecting the pain and horror he felt, and then he swung free, falling to the earth in a heap, his eyes glued to those of Jens Jergensen.

Now maybe they could talk peace. Now maybe Jergensen could explain to this brother how . . .

Looking at him, Jens Jergensen was moved with feeling, and he cried out to the staring Ute.

"You are a fighter, my brother. Und I think a good man, too. Ja, I vould like to . . ."

Jergensen's world brightened again and he was back in that strange beautiful country, but who were those people looking at him? They seemed to want something . . .

The Indian! He must see to the Indian, to help him.

He stood then, heaving in great gasping lungfuls of air, and when he at last staggered to the fallen Ute and grasped him by the shoulder to see if he could help him, the Indian's head rolled loosely and he slowly sprawled into the dust. Only then did Jergensen realize that the man was dead. Dead? But how could that be? He wanted only to stop him, to help him . . .

Slowly then he turned and it seemed to Jens Jergensen, the Danish Mormon immigrant, that night must be coming on. It was somehow getting darker, and for a moment he felt panic. But then he was in that strange country again, wondering where he was going.

His wife! He could see the face of the woman still in the wagon, and she was clutching his little daughter tightly to her bosom.

Why was she still there? In all this time she could have been miles away. He must get her out . . . must get her away!

He looked at her face again, but it was so far away, so very far away . . .

She was screaming! He could see her screaming something at him, but he couldn't seem to hear her because of those voices. They were close now, and they were calling him.

What could his woman be saying? There was nothing that could possibly be wrong now. Nothing. The Ute, that impossibly strong warrior, was dead. All that was left now was to get the woman and his little daughter out of this canyon and down to Uinta Springs.

If only he could get rid of this pain in his chest. It hurt so badly when he breathed. That and those voices, those voices that for some reason sounded so familiar as they called to him.

If only . . .

Why was the woman screaming?

"Voman . . . ?"

Something slammed hard against his back, something sharp and heavy, and he felt a momentary pain. And then somehow he was on his knees, his hands gripping the spokes he had set in his new felly so long ago.

It was getting lighter again, and he realized that his pain was gone. Why by golly, he felt pretty dang good! He could see his woman there before him, still in the wagon, only somehow she seemed to be drawing farther away.

And those people who were calling him. He knew that soon he would have to answer them. He couldn't ignore Kjersta and his parents. Kjersta? His parents? Why sure, they were there with his brother and sister, and that tall young man with them had to be his son, the son of him and the woman. He should have known! He should have recognized . . . !

He was dying! The Indians had killed him. Was this all there was to it? Why, there was no problem with this. It was . . .

He could see the woman again, his woman. Desperately he shouted to her, shouted with all his might, yet he could scarcely hear his own voice.

"My voman, you must save yourself und the child. I . . . now make you responsible for her safety . . . I vould do it if I could . . . Only through her vill ve be preserved! Voman, I vill vait . . . for you . . ."

He had never seen such beautiful country, nor had he ever felt such happiness. He waved to Kjersta and his family and walked toward them, feeling somehow lighter than he had ever felt. Already he missed his young wife and daughter, but when he turned to look at them again they were gone. Smiling then he continued on his way. It didn't matter, really. They would be together shortly. They would . . .

CHAPTER FOURTEEN

Christian Kjerulf pushed his head off the earth and blinked, trying to steady himself. He could see again, and he felt no pain. Where was he, and what was he supposed to be doing?

Then, as if from a great distance, he heard the screaming again, and suddenly it all flooded back to him.

He had to get to Brother Jergensen, to help him throw off that Indian!

Struggling to his feet he focused his eyes on Jens Jergensen and was relieved to see him on his feet and walking toward the wagon. He had gotten away then. Good. He had made it. He . . .

Suddenly he realized that another Indian was there too, one with a red gash across his head. The Ute he had seen on the ground!

Only now he was up and moving drunkenly after Brother Jergensen, his hatchet arching high in the air above his head.

That was why the woman was screaming. She was trying to warn Brother Jergensen, to tell him of his danger. But why didn't he listen? He was not even turning around.

Christian himself tried to yell, but he couldn't. There was no air . . . no air in his lungs to yell with. What could he do?

Desperately he looked around searching for some weapon. Then he saw the pitchfork. Stumbling he made his way to it, grabbed it up, and turning he moved after the hatchet-swinging Ute.

Hurry, Christian! You've got to hurry faster, he shouted silently to himself. But it was so far . . . and he was so tired.

The Ute was almost upon Brother Jergensen!

He must throw it. That was it. If he could throw the pitchfork like a spear . . .

With the last bit of energy the young man would ever possess in this life he drew back his arm and hurled the pitchfork. His momentum carried him a few feet farther before he crumpled to the earth, and he never knew if his throw was accurate, for Christian E. Kjerulf, hopeful pride of Sanpete Valley, was dead.

The pitchfork, however, did its job, though just a little late. Tutsegavit never knew what hit him, and he was long dead when the body of his victim, Jens Jergensen, fell slowly back across him.

Everything was suddenly, strangely silent. A lonely wind whipped at the grass and whistled through the canvas covering of the wagon. Somewhere on the hill a stone broke loose and rolled down the mountain making little cracking noises as it fell.

Overhead a buzzard circled in the brassy sky, round and round, as it floated on the wind, and its shadow crossed the canvas wagon top again and again.

One of the oxen switched its tail at a bothersome fly, and the woman knew she had to do something.

But what could be done now? Where could she go? Everyone was dead, even the Indians. This whole thing was like a bad dream. Her husband, so big and so strong . . .

The pounding of hoofbeats brought the woman back to her senses, and through a tear in the canvas she saw a lone Ute riding nearer on Terkelsen's big red stallion.

She had to get out! She couldn't let the Indian find her and the baby in the wagon! She'd seen too much before to let . . .

Jerking up the canvas on the side opposite the rapidly approaching horseman the woman leaped out and grabbing the baby she turned and ran.

Paralleling the wagon and about thirty yards away was a shallow ravine or arroyo, the same one that Jens Terkelsen had run down in his futile bid for freedom only a little while before.

The woman too reached the ravine unseen and sliding down its steep bank she stooped over and began running, the tiny baby clutched tightly in her arms.

She had run perhaps thirty yards along the twisted course of the ravine when she heard a savage shout from near the wagon. Glancing back she clearly saw the Indian paused on his horse, his rifle aimed directly at her. Involuntarily she cringed, waiting for the impact of the bullet. But there was no explosion and no impact, and when she looked again he had lowered the rifle and was now urging the stallion in pursuit.

Desperately she turned this way and that searching for a way to escape. What was she to do? She must get rid of the baby. Then at least it would be safe. She must hide it! But where?

There! There before her in the side of the ravine was a large hole . . . a large badger hole. It looked big enough . . . It had to be big enough!

Quickly she ran to the hole and thrust the baby, wrapped tightly in her blankets, into the hole. There was plenty of room. Now to seal the hole with a rock . . . There . . .

And now to run, to get as far away from that hole as she could. The Indian hadn't seen the baby, she was certain, so if she could just get away . . .

CHAPTER FIFTEEN

Hoskoots chased the red stallion back and forth up the canyon for fully twenty minutes. The horse would run a little way, pause to graze, and then slowly walk away as Hoskoots approached, keeping always just out of the range of his rope. To the stallion it was an old game, but the Ute found the experience terribly frustrating. At last, though, Hoskoots cornered him in a little cul-de-sac in the hills, and it took him another ten minutes to get back to the wagon.

Thirty minutes. It was really not a very long time, but for Ankawakeets and Tutsegavit it was longer than all the rest of their lives.

As he approached, Hoskoots noted with interest the stillness of the scene. The only movement was the constant switching tails of the oxen as they sought the destruction of the horde of stinging flies that harassed them continually. As the Ute cautiously approached he thought at first that the others, his friends, had ridden off leaving him behind.

That would be like them, but it mattered little to him. Only they didn't seem to have looted much, they hadn't burned the wagon, and why was Ankawakeets' horse grazing up there on the hill?

Something was wrong here . . . Terribly wrong . . .

It was then that he saw the bodies, and Hoskoots drew up the stallion in fear and amazement. There were four bodies here, as there should have been. Thing was, two of them were brown, dark brown, and as he carefully drew nearer he recognized them.

Tutsegavit and Ankawakeets.

Ankawakeets! But how could the giant Ankawakeets be dead?

Where was Namowah? Where were the bodies of the woman and the thin old man he had shot off the stallion? Something was going on here . . . something very strange!

Urging the horse around the wagon Hoskoots suddenly spotted a splash of color, a movement where none should have been. With a shout he recognized the woman, who was even then fleeing down the ravine.

At his shout she paused and Hoskoots threw his rifle to his shoulder, drew a quick bead, and pulled the trigger.

Instead of the explosion he had expected he heard only a tiny metallic click. He had forgotten to reload his rifle!

Hastily he poured in the powder and tamped it down, his eyes meanwhile searching for sign of the woman, who had suddenly disappeared.

When the rifle ball was in and tamped down he kneed the stallion and started after the woman. He thrilled with the responsiveness of the great red horse as it almost lunged out from under him. Kiyii, what an animal! He, Hoskoots, was now master of all!

Suddenly the woman reappeared, twisting and turning as she fled down the ravine. For a moment he held back, recalling her power over him the night before. Did he really want to go after her? Then he looked down at the stallion and remembered the words of old Tackwitch, that upon this horse he would be safe for the rest of his life.

What had he, Hoskoots, owner of the red spirit-stallion, to fear from a woman, witch or not? Why, she would be good sport for his rifle, very good sport. Of course he might miss, but it mattered very little, for in that case he need but run her down with the red stallion. She really presented no problem to Hoskoots except as a challenge to his ability with a rifle.

Still, if she were really a witch . . .

Hurriedly he pulled the stallion to a sliding stop and threw his old rifle to his shoulder. He could only see the woman part of the time as she bobbed along the uneven bed of the ravine. But that was enough. It was actually more than he could see of the long-eared jackrabbits he occasionally shot for food.

Steady down now . . . There, now just a bit . . . farther and a little bit higher . . . squeeze the trigger . . . just a bit . . . Now!

There was a tremendous explosion and Hoskoots hurriedly reloaded, waiting for the smoke to clear. As it dissipated he could no longer see the woman nor could he detect any movement whatsoever.

Had he missed? Was she hiding? Or had she perhaps taken herself away by magic?

Of its own volition the stallion started eagerly forward so that in a matter of seconds Hoskoots found himself gazing down upon the body of the woman.

She was lying crumpled amid the boulders on the bottom of the ravine, blood seeping slowly into the sand from the wound in her head.

It was strange how small she looked sprawled out like that on the bottom of the wash. How could he have ever imagined this woman to be a witch? She was simply a girl. A dead girl.

Hoskoots felt a sense of satisfaction and pride with his shot. Where was Namowah so he could tell him about it? It was one of the best shots, of a certainty, that he had ever made. Yet in a way he was sorry the woman was dead. He had begun making plans for her, and now her sudden death spoiled them. The woman had died too quickly . . . far too quickly.

Dismounting he wrapped the reins around a bush and then leaped into the wash. Here with his razor-sharp knife he quickly scalped the woman, removing a three-inch patch of hair and skin from the top of her head and leaving a spot of white skull exposed to the afternoon sun.

Again Hoskoots felt a twinge of doubt. This little body, this little woman, surely did not look or feel like a witch, but then how did one tell? Were not Tutsegavit and Ankawakeets dead? That could only have been accomplished by witchcraft! Hoskoots knew that to be true. And if she had killed them, might she not also come back for him? Hoskoots was glad he held her scalp in his hand. He wanted no more trouble with her.

Hoskoots the Ugly One was a very practical warrior. He now had the giant red stallion, the spirit-horse. Upon that animal he would be invincible in battle. Add to that the scalp of the witch-woman and the scalps of the other two men back at the wagon and he would be known far and wide as a powerful man, a very powerful man indeed.

As the Ute left the still form in the ravine and climbed up onto level ground he became aware for the first time of the attitude of the stallion. The animal was skittish, and was standing with its head up and its ears pricked forward, alertly watching the draw from which the Utes had attacked the wagon.

Could the animal see something? Or was it perhaps his sense of smell that warned him of possible danger? The breeze was coming from the draw toward them, and though Hoskoots did his best he could smell nothing unusual. Nor could he see anything. Mounting he slowly walked the animal across the rocky bottom and up into the mouth of the draw, his rifle ready and his own senses keenly alert.

What was it the red stallion had sensed? There was nothing . . .

Suddenly the horse shied and the Ute saw for the first time the body of Namowah his friend. He was dead . . . he had been killed by an arrow . . . a Ute arrow!

For the second time in as many days the Ute felt real fear, a slow crawling fear that gripped his stomach and paralyzed his thinking.

What demons had been at work here?

That arrow was a Ute arrow, but such a one as he had never seen before. Unless . . . He almost remembered something then, almost. But after a few feeble grasps his mind gave it up and he remembered nothing. He was convinced he had never seen an arrow like that before.

The witch!

Was that woman then truly a witch? If she were, then how could he have killed her? Quickly he looked to see if the scalp were with him, and as he touched it he felt a little reassurance.

But wait. Maybe she had allowed him to take her scalp to lull him into a false sense of security. Maybe she wasn't dead, but had come and killed Namowah. Maybe . . .

He had to go back. He had to go back and see if she was dead. Only in that way could he be certain . . .

All of them dead. All dead but him. Suddenly he thought of Tackwitch and of the little papers. He had been right. The wrinkled old man had been right. Only he, Hoskoots, the one who rode the red stallion, had been protected.

Cautiously he turned the stallion and retraced his steps back to the ravine.

Right ahead was the place. The witch-woman was sprawled on the rocks just around that bend. There, right down . . .

Hoskoots gasped in terror and amazement. There were the rocks on the bottom of the wash, but no woman lay upon them.

Hastily he glanced around, hoping against hope tnat he had come to the wrong spot. But no, this was it! Besides, there on the sand was fresh blood, blood from the hole in the woman's—no, the witch's—head.

He had to get away! She was near here, and she would be back for him. His only safety was upon his horse. He must not dismount!

Hurriedly he reined the red stallion around, and as he did so he heard, from the hills above him, the most inhuman and unearthly scream he had ever heard in his entire life.

In terror he started backward with his snorting horse, staring upward toward the source of the scream. Suddenly a strange object came hurtling out of the brush to flop awkwardly through the air and slam with a solid thump into the rocks at the base of the hill.

Hoskoots stared in terror at the mutilated body, knowing instantly who it was, or had been. It was the tall thin old man he himself had shot from the red horse.

How had he got up the hill, who had killed him, and above all how had he come sailing down again in such a strange and frightening manner? These were grave questions to the terrified Hoskoots.

Who could possibly have done this thing? Hoskoots cringed in terror as he stared at the body, but there were no answers, no answers at all.

He was alone! All were dead except him . . . Except him and the witch-woman!

But the old man was scalped. Would the witch-woman do that?

Suddenly it came to him, and Hoskoots stared in silent terror at the darkening hillside. The witch had scalped now because she had herself been scalped! There could be no other reason.

There was no other reason! It was revenge, and her next victim would be Hoskoots!

What was he doing here? Why had the red stallion lured him on as it had done? How could old Tackwitch have sent him on such a fool's errand?

He thought again of the paper, the tiny paper. Had his friends' names been written? Had his?

How he wished to run. Oh how he would have liked to send that great stallion flying away from that canyon of fear and spirits and witches.

But no, he would not! As long as he rode calmly and with dignity upon the back of the red stallion he would be safe. He must go slowly and show the witch no fear.

Carefully he rode past the wagon, where he paused just a moment to raise his arm in salute to his fallen brethren. He would have liked to take them with him.

On again, slowly, carefully. Ah . . . at last the cedars. Casually he glanced back at the wagon standing lonely on the sharp edge of the afternoon shadows. A breeze tugged at the canvas corner of the wagon cover, flapping it a little, and the heart of Hoskoots stood still.

The witch-woman?

There was a noise down there too, a faint crying noise. It couldn't be, he knew that. Yet it sounded strangely like the crying of a tiny baby. Another form of the witch-woman?

The big red stallion at last carried the Ute across the ridge and out of sight of the canyon and the wagon. Relieved, Hoskoots was just feeling the horse's rump muscles bunch together as the stallion set itself to run when his sharp eyes caught a movement up in the cedars, a movement where there should have been none.

For only an instant he held back, paralyzed with his fear of the witch, but then he plunged his stallion down the hill.

But for Hoskoots that instant was too long. It was forever too long. As the big red horse bunched its mucles to plunge down the hill a feathered shaft sped from the privacy of the cedars and with the fury of ten thousand angry hornets buried its terrible stinger in the throat of the uncomprehending Indian.

For a split part of a second time was suspended and Hoskoots gazed with horror at the quivering feathered shaft and at the red blood . . . his blood . . . that was quickly staining it a dark crimson.

He had been deceived! Tackwitch had lied! This was no spirit-horse. He had been promised that on this horse he would be protected until the day he . . . died . . . ?

Oh no . . . That was no kind of a promise . . . That was not right . . .

He had been killed!

He . . . Hoskoots . . . the Ugly One . . . was dying . . .

Chipetz . . .

Suddenly he remembered the name that had been evading him all day. The name of the owner of the arrows, he who had killed Namowah, scalped the old man, and now killed him, at last came to him. It was he who lived but was dead!

With his last breath he uttered the name, not once, but twice. And he said it loudly and distinctly.

"Inepegut! Crazy Man!"

Slowly he slid from the back of the stallion, the big red stallion, his wealth, and then he found death, that for which he had lived his entire life. The horse, skittish anyway with the smell of blood, reared back at this new development, wheeled, and fled away over the ridge. The stallion had had enough of death, and in a day or so it would wander into a corral near Nephi where it would be found and identified.

Meanwhile only silence reigned in the shadow of the cedar-crested ridge. A late afternoon breeze, lonesome for company, whispered through the grass and tugged laughingly at the long black hair of the Ute. Getting no response it gave up and moved on, leaving the Indian lying silent and still, alone on the lonely ridge above Salt Creek Canyon.

CHAPTER SIXTEEN

"And should we die, before our journey's through, all is well, all is well.

"We then are free, from toil and sorrow too . . ."

Groggily the woman shook her head, trying to clear her thinking, to cast out those lines from the Mormon hymn that kept spinning through her semi-conscious mind.

Oh how her head hurt! The pain was unbearable. She had never felt such pain before, nor had she known that anything could hurt so much.

Was she dead? Was this what it was like to be dead? No, she couldn't be. The pain was too real and too intense for her to be dead. Jens had said that in death there would be no pain, only joy and happiness.

Jens! Where was Jens? Where was she, and what had happened?

Oh the pain in her head! Groggily she shook it again, trying to open her eyes to see where she was. But they were closed fast and the effort was too great, too hard to bear. Maybe she was blind.

Unreasoning terror seized her and with all her concentration she brought a hand up to her face, a hand that seemed curiously detached from the rest of her body and yet remained somehow still under her command.

Fumblingly she rubbed at her eyes to find them coated with some hard sticky substance. Desperately she rubbed, but then her hand fell away as her whole body seemed swept around and around in ever darkening circles.

She was hot, so very hot. It must be the sun. She was in the sun, and somehow she had to get out of its light, into the shade.

Crawl! Move along! It is getting cooler, cooler.

Reaching out she felt the bank of the ravine, and with her hand she felt and knew that it was an overhanging bank. Struggling, desperately struggling, she wormed her way under the overhang, into the blessed coolness of the shade. She should crawl farther, but oh how her head was hurting.

The pain and the spinning! She was spinning around again, falling away, falling away. Grab onto something! Hang on!

Darker and darker and . . .

Someone was crying. Someone very far away was crying. On and on the piteously forlorn sound went. How could anyone cry that long? Would it never stop? Would it never . . .

The *baby!* It was the baby crying! Well, let Jens get up and take care of it. He always did it anyway, so that all she had to do was feed it. So let Jens go take care of her. The woman was just too tired to get up, just too tired.

Jens?

Sudden awareness came to the woman and she wormed her way from under the overhang and struggled to her knees where she swayed drunkenly back and forth.

She had to get to the baby, get her out of the badger hole and away from here, away from the Indians.

The woman remembered now the Ute who had chased her, and instinctively she raised her hand to the top of her head. In horror she jerked it away, a sudden wave of nausea sweeping over her as she realized that she had been scalped.

It was horrible beyond belief, and for a time she was unable or unwilling to accept the sickening realization as fact.

Yet she had heard of this before, of people being scalped and still living, but even in her wildest nightmares she had never dreamed it might happen to her. Never!

The baby. She had to get to her baby. The crying was more jerky now, and the woman feared she might be suffocating in the hole. Desperately she rubbed the blood from her eyes and struggled to her feet.

One step was all she took.

Then she was on the ground again, another wave of dizziness engulfing her.

She would have to crawl! Carefully she began to inch forward, picking her way around and over the rocks and boulders that lay in the bottom of the ravine.

It was still light enough to see even though the sun had set. As she crawled the woman wondered whether whole days had passed or whether it had been just a few hours since the massacre.

Massacre!

What a strange word. How clearly she could hear Jens Terkelsen saying that they would all probably be massacred, only saying it in such a sarcastic manner that she knew he was laughing at the idea. Now it looked as if he was the only one who had escaped. The woman wondered if he was laughing now, thinking about the massacre.

How could a silly little word like that ever describe all the blood and pain and suffering and sacrificing that had happened here in this little valley of Salt Creek? The word seemed to make such a futile effort . . .

The crying of the baby was getting closer, and the woman grasped the rocks and pulled herself forward along the twisting ravine. Every movement was torture, and quickly she lost all conscious thoughts of survival. Thoughts of the baby even retreated more deeply into her mind and she became conscious only of reaching that one rock just ahead. There, now just a little farther on, that rock over there. It must be reached next. Go! You can do it! Crawl! Now that piece of driftwood. See it? Crawl again. Keep crawling, crawling . . .

She had to get the baby out of the hole, get her out before that hole became her grave. Each movement was torture, each foot gained was a monumental effort of endurance. It would never end. She was not even moving forward. She was . . .

Suddenly the woman realized that the sound of crying was coming from directly above her. Haltingly she drew herself up to the badger hole, where with desperate trembling fingers she clawed out the rock and then the sobbing baby.

As one in a dream she squatted on the floor of the ravine, tore open her blouse, and held the tiny infant close against her swollen breast. Quickly the child's sobbing subsided and she was gurgling and suckling contentedly on the warm milk of the woman.

Numbly she watched the child, her mind closed and blank against the pain in her head. Never had she experienced such pain. Why wasn't she dead? It would be so much easier to be dead, and . . .

There was blood on the baby!

Frantically the woman rubbed it off, searching with anxious fingers for the wound on the tiny child. After several seconds the woman suddenly realized that the blood did not come from the child. It was dripping from her own head, and it was dripping rapidly, too rapidly. If that bleeding kept up the woman knew that in just a short while her strength would be gone and she would bleed to death.

Well, let it happen! The sooner the better. She had wanted to die for a long, long time, and now here it was right before her. She would be foolish to fight it. Besides, the pain was so bad that she was certain she couldn't stand it much longer. Why, all she needed to do was lie back, close her eyes, and . . .

"My voman, you must save yourself und the child! I now make you responsible for her safety. I vould do it if I could. Only through her vill ve be preserved."

Startled, the woman jerked open her eyes and stared around into the gathering twilight.

Jens? Was that Jens? Had she heard him?

But no, she couldn't have. Jens was dead. She had seen him die!

But it sounded so real, so real.

Wait a minute. Now she knew. Just before he died, as he clung to the spokes of the wagon wheel, he had spoken those exact words to her. That was it. She had heard him, all right, but only in her memory. Her mind was playing tricks on her.

Still, it seemed so real.

Dazedly she leaned back and closed her eyes. She was so tired, so very, very tired. She . . .

"My voman, you must save yourself und . . ."

Oh no! Not again!

"Jens," she sobbed, "leave me alone. Please just leave me alone and let me die. I am so tired, and you can't know how badly my head hurts. Just leave me be. You have no hold on me any longer."

The woman then struggled to her feet, turning back and forth, staring into the gathering twilight of early evening, searching for sight of her husband, whose voice she seemed to hear so clearly.

But there was nothing to see, nothing at all. The hills above the ravine were black with shadow, and the wagon, across the rocky bottom, seemed simply a lighter shadow against the blackness of the hills beyond. Nothing moved, and the silence of the canyon was deafening in its magnitude and intensity.

Suddenly she screamed, loudly she screamed, relieving all her pent-up emotions. But her only answers were the echoes the silent canyon returned to her.

Slowly then she closed her eyes and sank to her knees in the rocks again, and as she did so there swam before her mind, as if in a red haze, the vision of her husband clinging to the wheel spokes as he looked up at her. And again she could hear his voice, strangely soft and yet so vividly, as he pleaded with her.

"My voman, you must save yourself und the child . . ."

Tears came suddenly to her eyes and the woman bent double as she held her tiny child to her bosom and poured out her anguish and her grief to that God in whom Jens had placed so much confidence. It was perhaps the first real prayer she had ever offered, certainly it was the most sincere, yet it was more sobs than words. Jens had told her, many times over, that God was always listening, a God full of love, understanding, and compassion, who was always willing to help those who had finally reached the limits of their ability.

Slowly the intensity of her grief subsided and she experienced the beginnings of a feeling of peace and well-being that was to sustain her through much yet to come.

Softly she sobbed into the deepening shadows while the baby, contented now, fell into a fitful sleep.

Quietly the night breezes stirred through the grass along the sides of the ravine and whispered through the needles of the spruce and pines high on the slope. The creatures of the night began to stir, and as the brilliant moon crested the ridge to the east a lonely coyote raised his nose to test the wind, voicing at the same time his plaintive sentiments to the silent granite ramparts around him.

The woman, at last lost in an uneasy slumber, was only dimly conscious of the yelping coyote. A little later when he yelped again the sound was much closer and the howl brought the woman to full consciousness. She realized then that she had to move.

Her sleep had not been restful but had been disturbed by a horrible dream that kept repeating itself over and over. She would be chasing Jens, trying so hard to catch him, and she would almost get to him when he would turn around and it would not be Jens but an Indian standing there grinning at her. Then it would start over again.

The coyote yelped again and then another joined in, and they were very close, very close indeed. Suddenly the woman realized why and in horror she started to her feet to drive the wily scavengers away from the bodies surrounding the wagon.

Haltingly she moved out of the ravine to stumble across the gravel flats toward the wagon, her baby unconsciously clasped in her arms. It was difficult to think, to focus her mind on any single thing other than moving one foot before the other. Somehow she drove the yelping and snarling prairie wolves away from the wagon and the snorting oxen. Then, acting now solely by instinct, she gathered together the makings of a small fire. Somehow she kindled it, and as the flames licked slowly to life she collapsed against the wheel of the wagon.

It was only then that she became aware again of the baby, that tiny creature that was trusting so completely in her. But it was too much to expect, too much . . .

Gradually the flames ate higher into the pile of brush and limbs, and as its spectral light flickered past her the woman caught her breath in terror. There, almost at her feet, lay the body of her husband sprawled across the dead Indian who had finally killed him.

With a sob she lunged to her feet, but as she did so she caught the gleam of the fire in the open eyes of her husband, and she knew that she must close them. Somehow it did not seem right that a man could be dead and still have his eyes open. Carefully she reached down and pulled the eyelids closed, and as she did so the lines from an old poem ran through her mind.

> . . . 'e pulled the shades
> on the windows to her soul,
> for the light was out
> and the lass would be home no more.

For a long time the woman stood silent, unable to look away from the face of her husband. It was so tranquil, so serene, almost as if he were happy, almost as if . . .

She wondered where he was now, and if he had meant it when he said he would wait for her. Knowing Jens, she thought, meant knowing that he meant it. If only he were right and he could.

Later the baby began fussing again, and it was only while nursing her that the woman realized that the oxen were still chained and yoked to the wagon. She should free them to graze and rest, for they would need their strength.

It took more energy than she knew she had, but at length though still yoked together they were free of the wagon. For a moment or two they stood irresolute in the firelight, but then they turned as one and began lumbering back down the canyon, where they were quickly lost to view in the darkness.

Wonderingly the woman watched them disappear, astonished that they had left her so quickly. And what about the other livestock?

Where had all those other animals gone? Had Brother Terkelsen come back to gather them up?

No, he couldn't have, for he would surely have taken the wagon and oxen too.

The wagon and oxen! Oh no! In anguish the woman realized that she had just turned loose the only practical means she had of escaping from this terrible canyon.

But wait. Maybe she could catch them. Surely they would not go far, and it should be little trouble to lead them back, hook them up, and start the wagon going.

Stumblingly the woman started into the darkness after the oxen, but she had run only a few steps when she lost her balance and crashed heavily into a clump of sagebrush. Weakly she tried to rise, to get after the oxen. But the dizziness was back and she was spinning, spinning, spinning, and she had no strength to rise.

She clutched desperately at the baby girl, her baby girl, as she slowly spun in ever growing circles deeper and deeper into the velvet blackness of unconsciousness.

Awareness came slowly to the woman, an awareness punctuated with the constant throbbing pain that filled her head. As she struggled to rise the pain increased and she attempted to cry out, only to learn of her desperate need for water. Her tongue was swollen to where she could hardly move it, and her lips were cracked and bleeding.

To make matters worse the baby was fussing again, demanding that it be fed another meal. Though it was still dark the woman knew, by the chill in the air, a chill that seemed to permeate her whole being, that morning was near.

She had to have water. Not only for her own sake did she need it, but for the baby's sake also. It must have been hours since she had last nursed the child, yet she was experiencing none of the customary swelling that told her when the baby needed to be fed.

She was so thirsty! And cold too! Her whole body was shaking with chills. The fire had long since gone out and there was no relief there.

The wagon! In the wagon was a quilt she could wrap around herself and the baby.

There was water there too, a whole barrel of water lashed to the side of the wagon. But it was so far away, so far away. How would she ever get the strength to get clear over there, clear back to the wagon?

For a moment, a long moment, she knelt in the brush, mentally gathering together every last shred of strength she could find. Only there was just not enough. She could never . . .

"Voman, I now make you responsible for her safety . . . I vill vait for you . . ."

Wildly the woman looked around into the darkness. Where, oh where . . .

Struggling desperately she rose to her feet. But she was so weak and so dizzy, and she swayed so drunkenly, that she made only two steps before she fell to her knees.

Well, if she had to she would crawl to the wagon! She would crawl, by thunder, and she would get there too!

Jens, did you hear that? You just watch! You'll be surprised! He had made her responsible to save his baby. Suddenly, and with some surprise, the woman realized that she fully intended to do just that! She *would* do it, too! If it took the last breath she ever breathed she would save this baby.

Crawl. Crawl, but don't think of crawling. Don't think of anything. No, do think. Plan ahead. You won't make it if you don't think. Think of Jens. Do what he would have done if he had been here. He would save the baby, his woman knew that.

Grimly the woman determined to herself that she would honor his dying wish. She had honored him little enough while he had lived. So now was her chance to finally give him the honor and respect he deserved. She would throw out the past and forget it.

But wait a minute, another side of her mind asked. What about all that pain and sorrow that come with commitment? What about the vow you made to never suffer through that again?

Well, what about it? Can't a person change her mind? Can't a person admit that maybe she was wrong? Besides, nothing can hurt worse than you hurt now, so what have you got to lose? Yes, what have you got to lose? No, by thunder, Jens had given his all! If he's waiting, and he said he would be, then you'd best give all you've got too. Just so when you see him you can look him right in the eye, no flinching, and say, "Well, I did what you asked."

Perhaps it was too late to really matter. But Jens wouldn't think so. Nosirree! He was forever telling her that their marriage was eternal and would go on after death. He'd been right about everything else. He'd better be right about that too. Just so she could tell him that she'd done the right, the good thing.

"Jens!" she suddenly shouted into the darkness, her voice sounding high and squeaky. "Jens, you just watch me! I'm going to save your baby! Yessirree, I'm going to save *our* baby! I don't care what else happens, I'm going to do it! So tell God to help me and then set yourself down to watch, 'cause here we go!"

It was almost more than the woman could do, pulling herself up so she could reach within the wagon. But at last she did and her groping fingers found the dusty old brown quilt. And they found something else too. They found the sunbonnet she had taken off and tossed into the back of the wagon the previous afternoon.

The woman knew her head was bleeding again, and she suddenly realized that if she was to save her daughter she had to stop the bleeding. The bonnet would make the perfect bandage for the monstrous wound on her head.

Folding a rag she used for a diaper for the baby the woman placed it on her head and then tied the bonnet securely over that.

Then, because it wasn't until that moment that she thought of it, the woman removed the baby's soiled underclothes and put on clean ones.

The oxen were gone, she knew that, and so the woman knew too that if she was going to get out of Salt Creek Canyon she was going to have to walk or crawl. She shuddered at the prospect, but she had it to do and so, with the help of God, she would do it.

After a great deal of effort the woman got the lid off the water barrel. A little at a time she let the liquid trickle down her throat. Her father had taught her to do that when very thirsty. Gradually she increased the amount until in a few moments she had taken in a great amount of water, much more than she could normally have consumed.

The dizziness was coming again and the woman felt an urgency, a need to hurry. Hastily she searched for a canteen or any type of container to carry water in. But she could find nothing. She thought of food, too, but she felt no hunger and so she took none.

Clutching the blanket around her shoulders so it would cover both her and the baby the woman stepped resolutely away from the wagon, her destination Uinta Springs. She had seven miles to go.

As she passed the brush pile where her husband had fought the day before, something gleamed at her in the moonlight. Almost without thinking the woman stopped and picked it up. A knife. Her husband's knife! It was the one he had dropped during his battle with the Ute. With mixed emotions the woman slipped the blade into the sash of her skirt, and then she stepped determinedly forward. Amazingly she walked nearly one hundred yards before dizziness and weakness from loss of blood forced her to her knees.

It was growing light, and for the first time the woman thought again of the Indians. Could there be more? There was certainly the one who had scalped her. Would he come back?

She knew suddenly that she was close to unconsciousness. Where to hide? She had to hide!

In desperation she pulled herself up the hill and into a thick clump of oak. There were leaves here, lots of last year's leaves. She had to hide until she got a little strength back. She had to save the baby!

Pull the quilt over them! Scrape up leaves onto the quilt . . . Jens was counting on her . . . She had promised him, she had promised to . . .

CHAPTER SEVENTEEN

It was an hour past daylight before there was any movement in the valley of Salt Creek Canyon. Even then the movement was so subtle and so slight that most would not have been aware of it.

One moment the hillside was bare and empty of life, a rock-strewn slope where not even a clump of grass seemed welcome. The next moment one of the rocks seemed to have changed position, and was a little lower down the slope. Still, nothing seemed changed, nothing seemed different.

A little later the rock moved again, and still later a clump of grass at the foot of the hill swayed in the wind.

But there was no wind.

Again the silence, again the stillness. The only sound in the canyon was the buzzing of the flies in the warmth of the morning sun. A buzzard circled warily in the air above the abandoned wagon and Tabby, the sun, climbed steadily into the morning sky.

A tiny bird floated down from the hill to settle onto a clump of sage. Then just at the last minute it veered sharply away and with a cry of warning and alarm sped away to the south.

A moment later the form of a man seemed to materialize from the open ground beyond the sage. For a Ute he was very large, yet when he moved forward it was with all the stealth and silence of a great cat.

His face was flat and hard, his cheekbones high, and his eyes black, like others of his race. Yet in his eyes there was a difference too. It was not at once easily discernible but was nevertheless most definitely there. For in his eyes danced a strange light, one neither natural nor pleasant to witness, a light that seemed somehow repulsive to the few who had viewed it and lived to tell of it. In his eyes danced the lights and burned the fires of insanity.

He was Inepegut.

The Crazy Man.

He was the killer of Namowah, Hoskoots, Jens Terkelsen, and at one time, of even his own mother.

And he was angry. Crazy angry. He had chased the red stallion all night long and had never even come within fifty yards of him. Inepegut had never seen such a spooky horse.

He had wanted that horse badly, but when he could see that catching the stallion might mean another day or two he immediately abandoned the chase. The price, for Inepegut, was too high, at least for the present.

After all, he now had the wagon and all it contained, and the wagon was running nowhere. He would be wise to return and loot it before it was discovered by others. Then perhaps he would go after the red stallion.

He had invested much in obtaining that wagon, and he certainly was not ready to lose it to some chance happening.

He grinned evilly as he thought of lying on the hillside above that idiot Hoskoots. Even a fool would have known he was there, but Hoskoots had never suspected his presence, not even a little.

So now the Ugly One was e-i. He was dead, as were Namowah and all the others. Again Inepegut grinned as he thought of their deaths, deaths that he alone had brought about. Deaths that were perfect, swift and sure. Inepegut felt great pride in his work.

He was a master of his trade.

He was a killer.

And he would soon be the husband of Chipetz!

He knew the others thought of him as crazy, but that knowledge bothered him not at all. They were all fools, foolish creatures who were every bit as katz-te-suah as the strange whites who were coming with such alarming regularity into his land.

They all reminded him of poo-chump, stupid senseless lice that were worthy of nothing but extermination.

So Inepegut exterminated them. Red skin, white skin, it didn't matter. They were beneath him and so he killed them. As he would a snake or an insect he squashed them beneath his thumb, and he was called crazy because he did so.

It was Tabby-moushy, sunrise, when Inepegut first came to the brow of the hill and looked down on the wagon. The bodies were strewn about just as they had been the afternoon before, and there was no sign of life to be seen anywhere. Yet something bothered him. Something was wrong, was different than it should be.

Cautiously he approached. Inepegut, the Crazy Man, was in no real hurry. He had nothing more important to do with his time than to secure that wagon, and he felt no urgent rush to get it done.

Not when something was wrong. Not when he sensed a problem, a possible danger.

Especially not then.

He had seen a man once, one who was katz-te-suah, walk carelessly up to a dead body to take the scalp. Without warning that "dead body" had risen up and slain the foolish man and then escaped.

Inepegut never made that mistake. Caution was his law of good health, at least usually, and so he stalked the wagon as if it contained live enemies. For it still might.

From the barren slope he observed everything carefully. There was no movement, no sign of life. The bodies certainly looked e-i, and they were all as he had observed them the afternoon before after he had killed the old white man.

So what was bothering him? He didn't know, but he wasn't going any closer until he could determine exactly what was wrong.

The morning was still and Tabby was warm on the slope. A lizard scurried with heaving and panting breath from one sunny rock to another, a grasshopper bounded and clattered erratically past the still form of the Ute, and a little later a tiny bird spotted the Crazy Man and flew away in alarm. Still he remained immobile, his nearly naked body looking like nothing so much as a lumpy outcropping of rock, a natural feature of the slope.

An hour passed and then nearly another before the Indian gave up in disgust. There was absolutely nothing wrong. There couldn't be! There was no life and no sign of anything that might prove dangerous.

He stood then and strode toward the wagon, his alert eyes missing nothing as he moved forward.

Inepegut had not seen the actual fighting because he had been busy stalking the old man. Now, as he read the signs of the fight in the dust and dirt and looked more closely at the bodies, he was amazed. Amazed and impressed.

He knew Ankawakeets, knew of his great size and strength. Yet there he lay with his spine snapped in two as if he had been a bone doll the little ones had tired of playing with.

Inepegut laughed with glee at the humor of his comparison. Ankawakeets a bone doll. That was truly funny.

Suddenly, viciously, Inepegut kicked the body of the dead Ute, cursing him because he had been so stupid as to die so quickly. Why wasn't the Ute alive so Inepegut could tell him that he was no more than a bone doll. Tell him, and then kill him.

The insect!

Deftly then he removed Ankawakeets' scalp and moved on. Already the dead Indian was gone from his mind.

A trail of blood showed him how far the mortally wounded Christian had run, but Inepegut was not so interested in him as he was in the other white man, the one lying on the dead Tutsegavit.

The grinning Crazy Man set about examing the dead Jens Jergensen.

Quan-na e-i, the stink of death, was in the air, yet Inepegut paid it no mind as he sat and contemplated the white man.

This had been one real towats. He had been shot through the chest and the wound had been made some time before he died. He also carried at least three major stab wounds and Tutsegavit's quepannump or ax was still embedded in his spine.

Inepegut grunted in fear and amazement. This white man was narri-ent. Oo-ah, and katz-at myshoot-te-quoop too. Inepegut was glad this old one was dead. He was too strong, too full of bad medicine. It was little wonder the others thought of him as mo-ap, a spirit. Inepegut half believed they were right. It would not do to stay too close to this man, to this towats.

Cautiously Inepegut backed away from the body of Jens Jergensen, and as he did so his moccasined foot stepped directly into the white pile of ashes that remained from the woman's fire. Beneath the ashes were a few hot glowing coals, and as his foot came in contact with them the startled Crazy Man yelped and leaped away.

A fire!

Coo-nah!

How could there be a fire here when everyone was dead? Inepegut had made certain of that fact with the slaying of Hoskoots, the last and only survivor.

So who had come back to build this coo-nah? Might it have been built by mo-ap, a spirit? Possibly, but Inepegut had never heard that mo-ap needed fire.

But then who else? There was no sign of any other Utes being here. The wagon was untouched and there had been no looting. The oxen were still . . .

The oxen!

That was it! The oxen were gone! That was what had been bothering him all along. Somebody had been here, turned loose the oxen, built a fire, and then vanished. He had disturbed nothing, taken nothing. And he seemed to have left no sign of his leaving, no trail.

Inepegut crouched low against the ground, his eyes wide with fear. This was pe-ap myshoot-te-quoop! This was big medicine!

Suddenly and swiftly he placed an arrow in his bow and then rapidly he spun around several times, the bowstring taut and the arrow ready to kill. Only there was nothing to shoot at, nothing at all. The canyon was still, totally silent in the warmth of the morning sun. Other than the constant buzzing of the flies there was absolutely no sound. Total silence constantly barraged his ears with its emptiness.

Suddenly and without warning Inepegut screamed and leaped high in the air. From rock to rock he leaped, screaming as he jumped and waved his bow in the air with the arrow still held in position and ready to shoot.

Then just as suddenly as he began the Ute stopped and with incredible swiftness spun and released his arrow. There was a soft whirr and then a solid thump as the stone point buried itself in the heavy side of the wagon. For a moment the feathered shaft quivered with the impact, and then it too was still.

Inepegut stood silent and alone, sweat pouring down his face, his nostrils distended and his eyes wide and staring.

Slowly his heaving chest relaxed and his extended arm fell to his side. The bright fire faded from his eyes and Inepegut the Crazy Man dropped to the earth.

No one, be he man or spirit, had the right to come near this wagon, which belonged to him. Because some foolish person had now done so he would have to die. He, Inepegut, the great killer, would see to that. Furthermore, he would die slowly and with a great deal of pe-kon-gah.

Back and forth the insane Inepegut ranged carefully over the ground, his keen but muddled mind sifting and sorting out the confusion of tracks left in the dust of Salt Creek Canyon.

Time was as nothing, and the Crazy Man forgot even the wagon with its loot as he searched for clues to the one who had dared violate the sanctity of his spoils.

Within a little while Inepegut was certain that the one he searched for was a small person, perhaps even a boy. Yet this one seemed to be sick, for his tracks were erratic and frequently he crawled, leaving a handprint here and there.

Unless perhaps he too was searching for something. But what could that be? Might he have been reading sign as Inepegut was now doing? It was a possibility, and the Ute sat up and looked around carefully as he thought of it. Yet how could a boy know enough to search for sign? The whole thing was a puzzle, and Inepegut scratched his head with the perplexity of it.

Eventually he found the tracks leading from the ravine, and these the Ute carefully backtracked, approaching the arroyo with a great deal of caution.

He soon found where someone had squatted on the bottom of the ravine, and now he found the bloodstains on the rocks. This boy was not sick, he was wounded! That would make quite a difference.

Suddenly Inepegut noticed something else. A large rock lay over-turned on the bed of the wash, a rock that had not originally come from there. Quickly he looked around, and his eyes came to rest on the hole of o-num-buds the badger. There was soil on the rock. Soil that had come from around the hole of o-num-buds.

Why had this boy pulled the stone out of the hole?

Inepegut could tell that the hole was an ancient one, yet still he approached it carefully. The Ute had a massive respect for the fierce warrior o-num-buds, for badgers feared nothing and were always ready for battle, and expertly so too.

Cautiously he peered into the hole.

Nothing.

Next he slowly thrust in his bow, ready to jerk it back at the first hint of opposition.

Yet again there was nothing.

Finally, carefully, Inepegut inched his hand and arm into the hole.

Still nothing . . .

Wait a minute! The hole was wet. Or at least the earth inside the hole, along the bottom, was wet.

Carefully Inepegut rubbed his hand over the moist soil and then pulled it out. Mud. Slowly he raised the hand to his nose and sniffed it carefully, his eyes widening in surprise as he did so.

Urine?

But why would a boy make water in the old badger hole? Why

would he pull out the rock and then make water there? Furthermore, the size of his tracks indicated he wouldn't be large enough to do so at all. Not according to his tracks he wouldn't be.

So what was going on?

Again Inepegut scratched his head, trying to puzzle this mystery out, trying to make sense of a thing that made no sense at all.

Could it be that this creature he was following had hidden in the hole?

But no, that couldn't be! The hole was far too little for that. Far too little, unless . . .

Once again Inepegut looked nervously around.

Unless what he was following was indeed mo-ap.

Inepegut did not believe in spirits. And he didn't simply because he had no place in his thinking for them. He had never before seen any indication of their presence, and his life was such that he relied completely on his own abilities and never on outside help. Especially on outside help from something that he hadn't believed in.

But now he began to wonder if the traditions of his people might not be accurate. Nothing as big as a large boy could get into a hole as tiny as that unless he were mo-ap. At least not that he could see.

But wait a little. Over there it looked like more tracks or sign coming along the ravine. Moving cautiously Inepegut began to examine them.

Something had dragged itself along the ravine. Something . . .

Oo-ah, there was the print of a hand, the very same hand that had made the prints back near the wagon. Here was more mystery, but at least he could backtrack this kind of trail. That way he might learn just what he followed. Meanwhile he would forget about the hole.

Carefully he moved up the ravine, following the smudges and tracks along the bottom of the wash.

But now something else was bothering Inepegut. In several places he found in the sand the distinct prints made by loose clothing being dragged along or knelt upon. If he hadn't known better Inepegut might have thought those prints were made by the dragging of a . . . dress?

Could he be following a woman?

Sudden inspiration seized him and he leaped ahead to where he had seen the woman lying dead on the bottom of the ravine.

Gone! The woman was gone!

Inepegut suddenly grinned widely. The woman was alive and she was wounded. This was a great thing! She would be easy to capture, and then . . . Oo-ah, this was indeed a great thing!

Beads of sweat were already standing out on the Ute's brow as he leaped from the ravine and sprinted back to the wagon. He must find this woman quickly. He could already feel the ache inside him as he thought of her.

Oo-ah.

A hasty examination showed the wagon to be empty, and it was only minutes before Inepegut located the woman's tracks leading away from the wagon.

Now he would find her! Now he would . . .

He was already running along the tracks of the woman when he thought of the wagon and of the rifle.

Inepegut stopped abruptly, and turning he retraced his steps. With the woman as good as his he felt no need for any loot the wagon might contain. Yet he was certainly not going to leave it for anyone else. Not he. Not Inepegut. No one else was going to enjoy what rightfully belonged to him.

Grinning happily he chipped sparks into some tinder and soon a fire was burning brightly. Next he overturned the wagon and set fire to it.

For a few moments he stood and watched the fire spreading rapidly throughout the wagon. Then he turned and strode to where Ankawakeets' beautiful new rifle lay in the dirt. From the body of the dead warrior he took the powder and the shot pouch. Carefully he loaded the rifle, to-wudg-ka, and then he set out again on the trail of the wounded woman. Her, he would puck-ki. Her, he would kill.

But not quickly.

The trail was so easy to follow that Inepegut trotted along it, and as he trotted he smiled with anticipation, the strange light burning in his eyes.

Black smoke billowed upward into the still air from the wagon burning behind him, but Inepegut did not look back. In his muddled mind the wagon and those who lay dead around it had already ceased to exist. For Inepegut, the Crazy Man, all life and all thought were centered around finding the woman. That was suddenly all that had ever mattered to him, and he would be successful. He knew he would be successful!

Suddenly he stopped. What was this? Where had the tracks gone? No more tracks? But there had to be.

Back up, back up . . . Oo-ah, here they are again. Now go carefully, go slowly. Ah, there they turn and pass through the shallow wash. Follow them! Follow them toward the hill. Look beyond . . . What is there? Why would the wounded woman want to climb the hill?

There go her tracks . . . up into that heavy stand of oak. Could it be . . . ?

Up there, oo-ah, where the leaves are disturbed, last year's leaves, there . . . under that big pile . . .

Careful now . . . Steady . . . Go cautiously . . .

Oo-ah!

CHAPTER EIGHTEEN

The woman regained consciousness abruptly and with full awareness.

Jens was dead!

Jens was dead and she was wounded and alone, alone with her tiny baby to care for and protect.

It was too much! She would never be able to do it. Oh, if only Jens were not dead! If only he were here to help her and tell her what to do.

For a moment she panicked as she thought of the terrible scenes of carnage and bloodshed she had witnessed during the previous twenty-four hours. By the atrocious brutality of these red-skinned savages, the woman had been made a widow. Yes, and a widow with little chance of survival because she herself had been shot, scalped, and left for dead in the bottom of a wash.

Left for dead and left, too, with the caring for a tiny baby that seemed to do nothing but further reduce either of their chances for survival.

But she was not dead yet, not by a long shot, for the need to live was rising strongly within her. True, she was handicapped by the child, but then because of that child she was gaining the desire, the will, the strength of effort necessary to ensure their survival. For Jens, and for herself too, she had to save their little daughter.

Over and over thoughts of Jens flooded into her anguished mind, and burning tears came suddenly to the eyes of the woman, the first she had shed since the massacre. Burying her face in the folds of the baby's blanket she wept bitterly and unashamedly.

She had been such a fool, such a simpleminded and selfish fool. Why had she never recognized what a fine man Jens had been? Why had she never accepted his love, or given him hers? Oh, what she would give for a second chance, a chance to smile at him and show pleasure as he came in the cabin door. Or maybe all she needed was just a chance to laugh with him at the silly things they did and said. Or to smile and feel love and joy together as they played with the baby, the baby Jens was so proud of and so afraid of at the same time. How she could have helped him to learn to love their little daughter.

Why, these were just simple things, common ordinary day-to-day simple things. Yet to the woman, who had allowed them to slip past her undone and unfelt, these simple things suddenly meant more than anything else in all the world.

"Oh, Jens," she cried softly, "will you ever forgive me? Will you ever believe that I do love you? And your daughter too? You must believe! You must know that I am sorry. I could have made your life so happy and so . . . so contented . . . But I was selfish, oh how selfish I was . . . and now it is too late, too late to tell you or to show you of my love . . .

"But the baby . . . Jens, you must not worry about our daughter! I'll save her! I'll protect her, I promise you. And Jens, please wait for me like you promised. If . . . if I didn't have that to count on . . . I . . . don't know . . . whether I could make it or not Please . . .

"Oh God, how am I going to do it? If only you could make the Indian die, or lose my tracks or something . . . anything! I've got to save Jens's baby, and I don't know how . . . I don't know how . . ."

Suddenly the woman sat straight up, her prayer and her tears forgotten. She was frozen in terror. She dared not, she could not move. For to her ears was coming the sound of a man yelling and screaming. She knew instantly that the noise was coming from near the wagon, so very cautiously she pulled aside the old brown quilt that covered her and the still sleeping child.

An Indian, a nearly naked Indian, was jumping around waving his bow in the air and yelling his lungs out. The woman, at least partially accustomed to the ways of many of the Indians, was amazed and not a little frightened at what she saw.

That man acted crazy! There was no rhyme or reason to his antics. It was no dance, and what he was doing reminded her of nothing so much as a temper tantrum.

Suddenly he dropped to his knees and began to slowly crawl around. Then, after a moment or two he again rose to his feet and, stooping, made his way slowly toward the ravine.

Now that did make sense! He was reading sign, searching for

tracks, trying to sort out hers from the others. Cold terror gripped her heart as the woman realized that it would be only a matter of time before the savage found the tracks she had made, tracks she had made no effort to hide or cover up. Tracks that led directly to where she and the baby were hiding!

Once again tears burned her eyes and she sank back to the ground sobbing. It was too much! It was more than she could endure. The terror, the fear, the awful feeling of impending disaster that seemed to go on and on, why did it never stop? Why could she not have peace?

"God, please let me die," she pleaded. "Either me or that Indian. Or else make him lose my tracks or something, anything? I've got to have help. You don't care about the Indian! You can't, not when he and the others have killed Jens and Christian and maybe Brother Terkelsen too. And God, they were good men, with lots of faith in you. Why does it have to be me that lives when I have so little faith or whatever it is that makes a person good? All I want is to save the baby. I don't care much about what happens to me after that. But I have to save our baby!

"God, please give me the strength to walk. Then I can do it. I know I can! And maybe just a chance to kill the Indian, just a chance. I'll do the rest. I'll kill him and then I'll take the baby to safety. He shouldn't live anyway, not any more than me. Please, just give me a chance . . .

"Oh, if only I knew if you were there to hear me! How could Jens tell that you were listening? God, why don't you say something—or let me know somehow that you can hear me?"

Struggling to control her sobbing the woman pulled the quilt back and rose slowly to her feet. The Ute was still back at the wagon, so she knew she had a little time. Not much, but a little.

Her first move, she realized, must be to get away from this place, to get away and gain time by doing it. That could be done by covering her tracks, but the woman sensed that that would not be enough. She might be pretty good at hiding her tracks, but that Indian would be an expert at following them. She could not hope to lose him, but she did have one advantage he didn't have, an advantage she must use at every opportunity and to the fullest extent possible.

While the Indian would understand only partially the nature of the woman he was following, she in turn knew a great deal about him. True it was that she had never seen him before personally, yet because of what her father had taught her she understood a great deal about his abilities, his nature, his habits, his beliefs, and his superstitions. She even knew a little of his language that her father had taught her. True, the Utes he had known were from Colorado, but she expected that the language was probably pretty much the same. At least she hoped it was. Then too, she could observe him while she remained hidden. That was in itself a little help, at least psychologically.

Carefully now the woman looked around and planned, forcing her brain to focus, trying to think as the Indian would so she could do what he would least expect her to do.

He would know by now that she was wounded and losing blood. He would not know how badly she was wounded, but he would guess. The woman knew she had left a lot of blood back at the wagon. She knew too that her tracks wavered a great deal, so the Ute would probably surmise that she was pretty badly wounded and so follow her accordingly.

Regretfully the woman acknowledged to herself that the Ute was right. She was badly wounded. Yet suddenly her mind seemed to be working with amazing clarity. Furthermore, she was now standing upright and feeling no dizziness.

Could it perhaps be an answer to her . . .

No! It was merely a light-headedness, a feeling of euphoria or whatever that could not last long. She was certain of that. Yet while it did last she must take full advantage of it.

The Ute would expect her to go the easiest way. He would expect her to go downhill, moving slowly, as any wounded creature would do.

So, she would go uphill. And she would go as rapidly as she could and still leave no tracks. Reaching down she quickly piled the leaves into a small mound where she and the baby had lain. She then picked up a large stone and heaved it off down the hill at an oblique angle away from the wagon. The stone hit heavily about five or six feet down, bounced once, and then gathering momentum it slid and bounced and rolled through the trees and finally clattered to a stop in the wash at the foot of the hill.

Satisfied with the results, the woman then reached down, untied her shoes, and threw them as far as she could off into the trees. She had no fear of going barefoot. She had spent a good portion of her life without shoes and her feet were well hardened. And she knew

that bare feet leave less of a print, or at least one less easily distin-
guished because feet have no hard edges to make marks with.

Confidently then she gathered up the baby and stepped up the hill
onto the edge of a small boulder. It was lichen-covered but the
woman was careful not to spin or twist her foot as she quickly
moved to another rock. In that way the crusty growth was not disturbed but actually helped to hide the way of her passing.

Again she felt amazement at how good she felt. Her legs felt
strong and she had absolutely no dizziness whatever. But how long
could this false strength possibly last, she wondered. Certainly not
very long, and yet . . .

From stone to dead tree limb to stone she moved up the slope, zig-
zagging back and forth and yet always moving upward and away
from the wagon.

The air was warm but a breeze coming down the canyon helped
cool the woman as she moved quickly along. She knew that her
movements were not perfect. One with only a little skill could work
out her trail. All she could hope to gain by her efforts was time, just
a little more time to get her baby and herself to Uinta Springs and to
safety.

Carefully her eyes scouted the country ahead as she walked along.
Frequently she would go far out of her way to hide her tracks or to
confuse her trail. Grassy clearings she skirted, knowing her sign
would be very visible there. At another point she climbed far up the
hill in order to walk for a quarter of a mile on a crumbling outcropping of sandstone. Fleeing in this way was tedious and time-consum-
ing, yet the woman knew that the Ute would be forced to follow
wherever she went and so lose considerable time himself.

She must also make the Ute realize that he was facing an antago-
nist who knew what she was doing. She had to convince him that he
must be very careful as he pursued this woman. Only in that way
could she ever hope to keep ahead of him, to care for the baby and
still reach Uinta Springs.

For more than four hours the woman moved steadily ahead, covering almost that many miles while still hiding her trail. Suddenly
though she grew very, very tired and weak, so that each step became
in and of itself a major effort and a significant accomplishment. Yet
her dizziness did not return and her mind seemed to remain very
clear and alert, something that continued to surprise her.

Up and down, up and down her feet went. On and on and on and on. She was staggering a little now as she moved forward into the late afternoon. And now her head was pounding dreadfully and each step became a terrible jolting that filled her whole body with agony.

Yet the baby was again asleep after having nursed while the woman picked her way carefully across the hills and down the long winding ravines that would lead her ultimately, she was certain, to Uinta Springs and to safety.

So now the baby was no problem, but her strength certainly was. After each step she knew she would never be able to take another. Each step had become an agony that could not be endured. She was not able to hide her trail any longer. She wasn't even able to try. She could only stagger forward, forcing one foot to move ahead of the other, over and over and over again.

She realized that she had to do something, and she had to do it quickly. Her strength, so miraculously given, was gone.

Miraculously? Yes, the woman knew that now. God, Jens's God, who Jens said loved all his children, had given her the strength to come this far. He had heard her! Suddenly her soul was filled with an amazing joy that seemed to sweep away all her pain and weariness.

God *was* there! He had heard her! Jens was right about his faith and the woman suddenly realized that Jens *would* be waiting for her. They *were* sealed together for eternity! What a fantastic thought to consider! She would see him again, she would have the chance to show him . . . $\sqrt{}$

Suddenly she stumbled and fell to the earth. With a rush all the pain and anguish returned and the woman wept as she pleaded with God, the Father in Heaven whom she had finally found, to give her strength and show her the way to go. She knew she had to hide, yet where could she hide that the Ute could not find her? If it were only night. If it were only dark, then she might have a chance. But it wasn't! It was still at least two or three hours to darkness, and that was too long, far too long.

She estimated that the Ute was perhaps an hour or maybe even an hour and a half behind her, but that was probably stretching it. She had not seen him since the wagon and he could be closer, much, much closer than she thought.

With a lunge then she started to her feet and stared behind her. Nothing! She could see no sign of anything.

Where could she go? Where could she go . . . ?

Suddenly the woman found herself standing above a little sage-filled swale or tiny valley that had been entirely invisible to her until a moment before. Then into her aching mind suddenly poured the beginnings of a plan, an impossibly foolish plan, yes, but perhaps it would work. Stumbling then she hurried down into the shallow depression, out into the very center of it.

With fumbling fingers the woman placed the baby on the ground and then tore a small strip of white cloth from the hem of her petticoat. This she tied to the top sprig of a clump of sage where it would be plainly visible to anyone who might view the tiny valley, but not to anyone who did not come exactly there.

Desperately then she gathered a handful of small stones which she carefully arranged on the ground. Turning then she scooped up her baby and ran staggering up out of the swale and toward the steep slope of the mountain towering above her.

Carefully she ran, desperately trying to place her feet with care, yet frequently she stumbled and often now she fell heavily to the earth, jarring the baby, who was now crying fitfully.

Would she never find what she needed? There must be a place . . . Somewhere . . .

Twice she thought she had found what she needed, but both times she was forced to move on, to look more carefully.

Her head was now pounding dreadfully and her eyes were reduced to two pits of flaming agony. Her throat was burning with thirst and her lungs ached with the intensity of an explosion. She must rest . . . She must . . .

There! There was the place she had been looking for! If only she could now do what she had to do. If only her strength would hold out . . .

Placing the crying baby down she sank to the earth, where she lay, momentarily exhausted, tears streaming from her burning eyes and great choking sobs wracking her tormented body.

At last she forced herself to sit up and tear another strip from her petticoat. Then she dragged at the bush until she had pulled its uppermost branch into her hand. To this she tied the white strip of cloth. Suddenly, though, it slipped out of her hand and whipped up, throwing the cloth across and to the ground. Desperately she sobbed and tore away another strip. Then she dragged down the branch again and tied the cloth to it. When released it whipped back to its former position, where the late afternoon breeze fluttered the tiny piece of cloth around like a tiny flag.

Perfect!

Now more stones . . . Good! Now get the baby and move on about ten yards, to those trees . . . there . . .

"Quickly, woman, work quickly, but do it right . . ." she sobbed to herself as her fingers struggled with their task. Twice she dropped the knife before she was finished, despairing of her task. At last, though, it was done as well as she could do it, so taking up the baby she hobbled to a stony outcropping, which she began laboriously to climb.

With aching and bloody fingers she clawed at the coarse stone as she pulled herself and her baby, her precious little daughter, upward and forward, ever upward and ever forward.

Uinta Springs . . . How far away was Uinta Springs . . . ? She had to get to . . .

"Please, dear God, please help me," she sobbed as she climbed. "I've done all I can, so please help me . . ."

How badly she wanted to stop. She was so tired, so tired and ever so thirsty . . .

Can't stop! You can't quit now! Keep going, woman. You told Jens you would, so keep going! Keep moving. You have to keep moving!

If you don't you may never move again.

There! Now you are at the top. See, you *can* do it. Now get moving . . . get moving . . . get mov . . . in . . .

CHAPTER NINETEEN

Inepegut moved cautiously up toward the pile of old leaves, his heart beating rapidly and his eyes burning brightly with their strange light.

Carefully he held out the rifle and slowly lowered the muzzle toward the pile of leaves. Then savagely he jabbed the barrel in to the moldering pile to hurt and stun the woman, the squaw who lay hiding beneath them.

He knew she was there! The evidence of her piling the leaves over herself lay all around, and Inepegut was anxious to see her up close. He hoped she wasn't dead, but he actually gave little thought to that as he jabbed the muzzle of the rifle through the leaves and into her body.

Only . . .

Only somehow he had missed. Somehow the end of the aukage, the rifle, failed to find the woman. Furiously he jabbed the muzzle of the weapon again and again into the loamy soil, filling the rifle barrel with dirt but still finding nothing.

Inepegut shouted and screamed and kicked desperately at the pile of leaves, scattering them in all directions in the flurry of his temper. Yet still he found no one, no one at all.

The squaw was gone!

As suddenly as it had begun his temper tantrum ended and Inepegut settled again to the task of following the trail of the woman. He was careful now, yet his flurry of kicking had scattered leaves far and wide and had done much to obliterate any sign the squaw had left.

Patiently and carefully the insane Inepegut worked his way in ever larger circles around the place where the woman had lain. His face was an emotionless mask yet in his eyes there smoldered the fires of insanity. He worked in total silence, but every few moments he would lunge to his feet, his eyes burning brightly, and scream insults and vulgarities at the squaw who had so far eluded him.

At last he came to a disturbance in the leaves that he knew he had not made himself. Something, the squaw, had stumbled clumsily here, leaving a deep gouge in the turf.

It was the squaw. He knew it was her, and below a little way was another mark. She was going downhill, and it looked as though she was trying to run, to escape.

Oo-ah, yes, she was trying to escape from him. Te-we-ne! He would make haste. She could not be very far ahead of him, not wounded as she was. Why, the squaw was katz-te-suah. In fact he could not imagine how anyone could be so foolish. Why should she run? Why should she try to escape? It must be as obvious to her as it was to him that this foolish squaw would be quickly captured. Oo-ah, look at the trail she was leaving! Even a child could follow her trail.

With great speed the wily Inepegut ran down the hill following the scars and disturbances left in the leaves and the soil. Once he came to a place where a great chunk of wood and bark had been knocked from a tree at about knee height and he paused a little to wonder at that. How could the squaw have done such damage to the tree? She must truly be making great te-we-ne in trying to escape him.

Shortly he arrived at the bottom of the hill, where the sign he followed entered the wash. Inepegut did so too, moving quickly and easily as he followed.

Here the earth was gouged, there a stone was chipped, there a large rock had been knocked into a new place, and there . . .

But there was no more sign! Quickly he ran down the ravine, searching the bottom and both banks.

Nothing!

Wondering now, Inepegut climbed the bank and worked his way slowly forward between the wash and the hillside.

Still nothing!

Crossing over the wash he worked his way slowly back to where he had started, carefully examining anything that might show any sign of the passing of the wounded squaw.

But still he found nothing, no indication that she had gone that way at all. Inepegut was amazed! How could a foolish woman, this wounded squaw especially, simply vanish from the earth leaving no sign whatever that he could find? It was not possible. Somehow he had been tricked. He, Inepegut, had been tricked by this squaw.

Suddenly he squatted on the ground, held his face in his hands, and sobbed out his sorrow and grief that the squaw had tricked him. For fully five minutes he rocked back and forth, sobbing and moaning as he did so, a lonely pathetic figure sitting in the dirt and rocks of Salt Creek Canyon.

Finally he stood up and pawing the tears from his eyes he walked back to where the tracks had entered the ravine, wondering all the while why the squaw would not give up and submit herself to him.

Again he dropped to his hands and knees so he could more carefully examine the sign left in the wash.

Here the bank was scarred where she had slid into the bottom, over there was a long mark in the sand, there was a small stone that had recently been chipped, and down a little way was that large rock that had been moved out of place. It surely looked as though she had been here.

But wait a minute! How could she have chipped that rock, and where had that large stone rolled from? Inepegut glanced quickly around, but there were no depressions that might have held that stone, none at all.

Hastily he ran to it and picked it up. The stone was rough and covered with fresh chips and scratches, and there on one side were splinters and pieces of bark and wood, freshly broken from a living tree.

Instantly Inepegut understood. He had been trailing a rolling stone. He *had* been deceived! Again the squaw had deceived him.

Screaming his rage he smashed the stone into the bottom of the wash and then he raged back and forth kicking at stones, tearing up clumps of grass, and beating at the earth with his fists.

Finally exhausted he took up his rifle, the new rifle of Ankawakeets, and dragged himself back up the hill to where he had found the trail of stone. Methodically he began crawling again in ever larger circles as he cast about for some sign of the squaw.

She had been here! He knew it and so knew too that somehow she had moved away. In doing that she had left some sign of her passing. She had to have left some sign! It was impossible not to have. Everything left sign . . . except mo-ap, the spirits.

Inepegut did not believe in such things, or at least usually he didn't. But now suddenly he wondered, he truly wondered. Could the squaw be shin-ob mo-ap, a devil spirit?

Instantly Inepegut knelt up and cast his eyes round about him in fear. Could she be here, hiding somewhere and watching him? Could the shin-ob mo-ap squaw perhaps even now be laughing at him? Straining his ears he listened intently into the afternoon, hearing the sounds of insects and of the wind as it whispered through the trees and along the ridges of the canyon. Yet to the Crazy Man it no longer sounded like the wind but instead seemed to carry the sound of mocking laughter, the mocking laughter of the squaw.

Inepegut leaped to his feet and fled away into the thicket of oak, yelling and screaming his fear as he ran, his eyes blazing with their strange white light. He must flee this devil spirit squaw. He wanted nothing more to do with her.

Suddenly he stopped, arrested in his tracks by something dangling from a tree directly in front of him. Cautiously he approached the object to hesitantly take hold of it.

A shoe! A shoe worn by white squaws! Oo-ah, yes, it was a shoe worn by the squaw he was chasing. But what was it doing here? Why was it hanging in this tree? Curiously he examined it, soon finding that it was not tied to the tree but seemed only to have caught there. Wondering now he looked around him. Over there, under that dead limb, was another.

The squaw was barefoot! But why had she removed her shoes?

Of course! It was to hide her tracks! Suddenly Inepegut smiled, and then he laughed aloud. This explained a lot. The squaw was indeed crafty, but she was no shin-ob mo-ap. She was only a squaw, and Inepegut would have her yet!

Hastily he examined the area near where he had found the shoes, but as he expected he found no sign. He was certain now that she had thrown the shoes from near where she had piled the leaves. If so, then still he would find sign near there.

It came to him then that she had rolled the stone down the hill to lead him off. That in turn meant that, wounded as she was, she had still chosen to flee uphill where he would not expect her to go.

Turning then he ran back to the pile of leaves, where he stopped again to consider. How would the squaw do this? To leave no sign she would have to move carefully, probably stepping on stones and whatever to prevent footprints.

Oo-ah, like that stone over there! Inepegut dropped to his knees and carefully examined it. He wasn't certain, but it did look as though a bit of the lichen had been crushed. Dropping it he moved slowly up the hill, examining with care each stone where she might have stepped.

Ayiee, this squaw was a smart one. Nowhere could he be certain where she had stepped, yet for some reason he was sure that he was now on her trail. Oo-ah, that limb was moved slightly from where it had lain so long, and now the man called Inepegut the Crazy Man was absolutely certain. The squaw had come this way, and soon he would come upon her.

Still, one thing bothered him. If she were as badly wounded as he thought she was, how could she be walking this rapidly and this surely? Down in the canyon she had been staggering and crawling, but now suddenly she was walking and perhaps even running as though she were in perfect health.

Inepegut shivered a little as he thought of that. Maybe she was indeed mo-ap . . . But no, she couldn't be! She was a squaw, and she was to be his until he chose to kill her!

Oo-ah, now he was at the brow of the hill. Which way, he wondered, would she go? No, which way *had* she *gone?* Quickly he cast about for sign, and it took only a few minutes to determine her direction. The squaw was still going eastward, or at least she was right here. Yet the squaw never traveled in a straight line, and each time he thought he could guess where she would go and then leave her trail to hurry ahead he would find nothing.

It was exasperating to Inepegut, for always he was forced to return and patiently work out every foot of her trail.

Even that would have been all right except that Tabby, the sun, was getting ready for darkness when the world would be covered with the great wah bab, the shadow of to-can, night.

Inepegut had no fear of darkness, but in the darkness he could not follow a trail. At least he could not follow the trail made by this squaw, this squaw who seemed to know more and do more than it was possible for her to do.

So with growing impatience the Crazy Man followed the almost non-existent trail left by the woman. Rapidly the sun dropped in the west, the shadows grew longer, and the evening breeze freshened and bent beneath its cool breath the leaves of the trees and the green grass that sparsely covered the long hills above the canyon called Salt Creek.

Inepegut, however, was oblivious to all of this, for he had suddenly run into another problem. The trail he followed was becoming easier to read and he could tell that the squaw was tiring. But then her tracks had turned toward a huge outcropping of sandstone and simply vanished. Inepegut could not even tell if she had gone clear to the rock, though it was the most logical thing for her to do.

Angrily he made his way around the quarter-mile ledge, searching carefully for any sign she might have left. Finally, near where he would have guessed that she would leave the ledge, he found a clear footprint in the dust. It was, in fact, the clearest print he had seen so far, and that should have warned him. But it didn't, and so he felt his great unhappiness with the print.

For it was pointing toward the ledge. He had finally found where the woman had climbed upon the rock. Yet why here, so far away from where he had lost her sign?

For a few feet he backtracked her, but what sign he found indicated that his first impression had been correct.

Again Inepegut began his search, and in an hour he had gone completely around the ledge of stone. Nowhere had he found any other sign to indicate that the woman had left the ledge. But she had to have left it! She was nowhere on it, for he had made certain of that too!

What had he missed? The only tracks he could find at all were these prints in the dirt where she had climbed on the rock.

Inepegut looked at the sun and angrily screamed his rage. Tabby was about to go behind the mountain! He had to find the squaw, and he had to do it quickly. He would find her too! He would find her if it took the remainder of his life! But how was he to find her before to-can?

Turning, Inepegut angrily stalked down the trail, backtracking the woman to see if perhaps he might learn something. As he reached the bottom of the draw, though, he suddenly shouted in happy surprise. There was a footprint going in the right direction. Hastily he moved forward. Oo-ah, here was another and there was yet another.

He had been tricked again by the craftiness of this squaw. That was a simple trick, yet he had never thought of it. She was a wise one, but he was even wiser, for he had again found her trail, one that was now very easy to follow.

Trotting for the first time he moved up the hill following the wavering tracks. The squaw was tired, and . . .

Oo-ah, there she had fallen to the ground, and up there was a bloodstain on that rock. It would not be much longer now. The squaw had finally tired herself to weakness and exhaustion.

Tabby was gone now, but there was plenty of light left to see by. He would find her any moment. He must go carefully, yet he would go quickly too, for the squaw was at last to be his!

Her trail was so simple now, so obvious. Here she had climbed the side of another ridge, yet she had crawled more than she had walked. See, here was more blood on the ground.

Now the top, and here were her staggering footprints going down into that little valley, down into . . .

Wait a moment! What was that object fluttering on the top of that mahp, that high sagebrush out in the center of the swale? What could this mean?

Carefully Inepegut approached. A piece of cloth was tied to the mahp! And here on the ground were the woman's tracks. Oo-ah, and something else too. Inepegut dropped to the ground to peer more closely at the small grouping of stones.

Dazedly he shook his head and rose to his feet. Never in his life had he been so amazed or so confused. The stones, small rocks the squaw had gathered, were formed into an arrow. And the arrow pointed the way the squaw had gone, it pointed the way she wanted him to go!

But why? Why would she draw his attention here with the cloth and then point the way for him to follow? It made no sense, no sense at all. Unless . . . unless . . .

Inepegut shouted and leaped into the air. Of course! That was it! He now understood perfectly why the squaw had brought him to the brush and then shown him the way.

The squaw had finally realized that flight was hopeless. She had done all she could, gone as far as she was able to go, and now could move no farther. She now realized that it would be most sensible to give in, to give herself up to the great Inepegut. She had done her best to escape, but now she had given in. He had won! He, the great Inepegut, he whose name foolishly meant Crazy Man, was to have the squaw.

Oo-ah, yes, and she probably desired him now as badly as he desired her. That was why she was hurrying him onward. Oo-ah . . .

Shouting aloud to the woman to wait for him Inepegut sped along her trail, peering anxiously into the gathering darkness for some sign of the squaw. At last he could show her, he could use her and kill her at his leisure. The squaw was his, the squaw . . .

There, directly ahead . . . Another strip of white cloth fluttering in the wind . . . Oo-ah, now he knew with a terrible certainty that he had been right. She was showing him the way!

Was there another arrow here? Carefully he looked, and in the deepening twilight Inepegut could just barely make out the outline of the stones. Still, they definitely formed another arrow. A slight change in direction was indicated, down into those trees. That was where she would be. Inepegut knew she was there, she was there and waiting for him. She had shown him the way and now she awaited only his arrival.

Oo-ah, life was sweet, sweet indeed!

Heedlessly Inepegut sprinted along the woman's trail, caution thrown to the wind as his heart pounded and his eyes glowed brightly with eager anticipation. The first of the trees flew past and again Inepegut raised his voice in a shout of exultation.

But suddenly something seemed to tug a little at his foot and there was a soft whispering in the air. Amazingly agile, the wily Inepegut was already turning, already twisting his body in the air when the knife, tied securely to the tension-released sapling, whipped a wicked slice across the front of his thigh.

With a scream Inepegut crashed into the brush and trees, where he lay writhing and groaning and gripping his bleeding leg. Before long, though, he knew that the wound was not serious, and then he pressed leaves against it and sat staring silently into the darkness.

The squaw had done it again, and now Inepegut felt the beginnings of fear of her as a person. She was no mo-ap, but she was surely a crafty squaw. Inepegut knew that if he had been only a little less fast the knife would have ripped out his bowels and he would have been dead. He must be more careful. He would catch her, but he would go more slowly and catch her only when she was so weak that he would have no further trouble from her. Tonight he would rest. In the darkness it would be too dangerous to try catching her. But there was tomorrow; there was always tomorrow.

Slowly all things in the Sanpete night returned to normal. The sapling with the knife tied near the top swayed gently back and forth as the wind blew through the pines, the quaking aspen, and the oak thickets. Far down the canyon a coyote howled into the night as it stared at the burning embers of what had once been a wagon.

A bat fluttered overhead seeking a swiftly fleeing insect, and three-people, not fifty yards apart, lay silent in the night. One lay thinking of the squaw, one slept, however fitfully, and one groaned unconsciously in an agony of pain and thirst as she held her child and waited for an attack that she knew was coming.

It was going to be a long night.

CHAPTER TWENTY

The woman crouched in fear and agonized silence atop the rocky cliff listening to the screaming and the groaning of the Indian somewhere in the darkness below her. Desperately she clung to her baby and to consciousness. She had to keep alert. She had to be ready so that when the Indian found her she could make at least one last feeble effort at defense.

For the woman was certain her knife had not killed the Ute. That was too much to expect, though the hope surely had been there. However, she had slowed him down a little, she was sure of that, and now she must use the time she had purchased for rest.

If only she could.

She tried, oh how she tried. But the agony of her screaming muscles, her tormented mind, and the feverish fire of her monstrous thirst drove sleep away and left her hanging in the darkness somewhere between delirium and unconsciousness.

She seemed to be running, running, forever running, yet somehow she could not move her feet. She would look down at them and see that they were somehow bound up in wagon spokes and fellies. But for some reason that did not seem a problem and she would make no effort to free them. Instead she would just keep on trying to run, sobbing and groaning with the effort and yet never stopping, knowing that if she stopped . . . But what would happen if she stopped? Desperately as she ran she tried to think, to remember what would happen if she stopped, but it was too hard to remember . . . to think . . .

Now she was in a different place, still running, still carrying the baby . . . It was still in the midst of mountains, but they were changed somehow and she couldn't recognize them. Now she was running downhill, faster and faster and faster . . . it was easy now, going so fast down the hill. It was fun, and somehow the pain was gone and she was free and . . .

Oh no! There was a cliff ahead, a gigantic cliff, and she was going to run off the edge . . . ! Stop! Why couldn't she stop? Desperately she turned and twisted, trying to stop, trying to go back, but it was no use, no use, no use . . .

The air! Now she was in the air and falling. Down, down, down . . . She could hear herself screaming . . . falling . . . round and round and round . . . spinning . . .

What was below, down through the smoke? Fire? Oh no, not fire! Down she fell, spinning ever lower and lower. The heat from the fire was now ascending, getting hotter . . . getting hotter . . . Her mouth and throat were burning as she breathed into her lungs the fiery hot air.

Desperately she clawed at the smoke trying to go back, straining upward as she fell, straining to reach back to the cliff, to . . .

There was Jens, grinning down at her! Jens, Jens . . . help, please help . . .

The crying was louder now as she desperately reached out her hand toward Jens, pleading over and over for his help.

There, almost now . . . almost . . .

Her hand was almost touching his when she looked again into his face. Now she was screaming, screaming her terror, a hoarse scream that was almost silent. For the face leering at her now above the hand that almost touched hers was not Jens. It was the face of an Indian, the battered face of the Indian who had chased her out of the little draw so long ago.

Jerking her hand away she watched in horror as the Indian suddenly changed, was suddenly the crazy man who was following her forever through the mountains.

But there was no time to watch him further, no time to do anything at all, for now she was spinnnig into the flames, slowly spinning into the ever hotter heart of the fire.

Strangely, it was not bright, but her chest hurt as the intense heat scorched her mouth, her throat, her lungs, burning . . . burning . . .

With a jolt she hit bottom and rolled over on her side, staring up into the inky blackness of the night. For a long moment she was lost, uncomprehending, wondering where the fire had gone, wondering where she was and who was crying.

Gradually, though, her mind cleared and she struggled to sit up, thankful that it was only a nightmare she had suffered through.

The baby! Her baby was fussing . . . In the darkness she could barely make out the struggling form of the baby a few yards away.

Slowly she crawled to the child to pick her up and comfort her, amazed that she seemed so far away. The baby was sopping wet and the woman had nothing else to put on her. But wait, yes she did too. She had used her petticoats for flags, why not for a diaper also?

With numb fingers the woman slowly removed the soiled clothing from the baby, tore another large section from her petticoat, and tied it around the little child.

How tiny she looked! How tiny and thin! Sudden terror gripped the woman as she realized that the baby was slowly starving, slowly dying from lack of proper nourishment.

In anguish the woman clasped the fussing infant to her breast, her breast that even now was empty of the life-giving nourishment the baby so desperately needed.

Was this how it was to end? After all her effort was the baby, Jens's baby, to die because she could not feed it?

No! That must not happen! The child must live, she must live to preserve Jens's posterity . . . But how was the woman to keep her alive? How . . .

"Voman."

The voice was quiet, so quiet that the woman was not even certain she had heard it. Anxiously she looked around, peering into the darkness in a futile search for her husband. But there was nothing to see, nothing at all.

"Jens? Jens . . . ?"

"Voman, remember vat I taught you. Ven man does all he can, then is the time to turn to God. Ask, und you shall receive."

The woman stared into the darkness, unbelieving.

"Jens? Jens, are you there?"

The voice had been so quiet, so . . . tiny. Was it possible she had heard him, or was it her mind again, playing more tricks on her?

But draw up a minute, woman. Was that so important? What had she thought he'd said? When a man had done all he could, then was the time to turn to God. Well, she had done all she could, that was certain! She had flown until she could flee no farther, her body felt as though it was on fire she was so thirsty, and now the baby was starving to death because she had no milk. Her body fluids were simply too low to make any, and because of that the baby might die. She might die in spite of all she had done.

All right then, she would not question Jens. She would do as he said. She was beyond anyone else's help, she was sure of that. God was the only one left to turn to.

Besides, and the memory or thought came suddenly and unbidden, somewhere, sometime, Jens had told her that God waited anxiously to help His children, but was prevented from doing so because these same children lacked the faith to ask Him for help.

Why certainly! Now she suddenly recalled the scripture Jens had quoted. "Ask and ye shall receive, seek and ye shall find, knock and it shall be opened unto you." Suddenly that scripture made great sense. If she could only have the faith to instigate the action by asking God, He would be bound to somehow answer her request. It was that simple.

Now all her pain, her thirst, and her weariness was forgotten as the woman rose stiffly to her knees and poured out her soul to God, her Father who lived in Heaven. Her words were neither flowery nor beautiful, just a simple expression of faith and then a straightforward request for the means to save the life of her daughter so that Jens's righteous desire might be fulfilled.

When she had finished the woman squatted back on the ground, feeling surprised and pleased at the calmness that had spread throughout her body. Yes, she was still thirsty. Yes, her head still pounded dreadfully. And yes, her muscles still throbbed with weariness. But somehow she felt good. Somehow she knew beyond doubt that all would work out well for the baby as well as for her and Jens. It was truly a wonderful feeling.

CHAPTER TWENTY-ONE

Inepegut the Crazy Man sat quietly in the grove of spruce and aspen staring into the darkness. Occasionally he chuckled deep in his throat when he thought of the squaw and what he would do to her, and once or twice he even laughed aloud in gleeful anticipation. Mostly, though, he sat brooding in silence, angry that the woman had eluded him so far and hurt that she should continue trying to do so when it was so hopeless for her.

Already the gash on his leg was forgotten, forgotten in the anticipation of what tomorrow would bring. That would be his day, the day when he would finally reign supreme over the strange white squaw. If he could only wait for tash-a, if he could only wait for daylight.

But now his head, his tot-se-in, was hurting. That was not unusual, for ever since he could remember his head had hurt when he tried to think too hard. Yet now he was not even thinking, not even shum-i, and still his head hurt, pounding with a pressure that made it feel as though it would pop like a pocket of pitch in a hot fire.

At last Inepegut could stand it no longer. He rolled on the ground, he pounded his head against the soft earth, he struck his head with his fists, and finally he held his head in his hands while he rocked back and forth on his knees in his agony. Yet still the pressure held and the pain continued.

At last, to gain some kind of reassurance, he blindly reached out and groped in the darkness for his rifle, the new rifle that had so recently belonged to another. The aukage or rifle gave Inepegut great comfort. Always he could kill with his bow or his knife, but the rifle gave him a great deal more power. With it he could kill easily and from a great distance.

Perhaps that should be how he killed the white squaw. If he could only catch up with her then with his new rifle it would be a simple matter to kill her. Oo-ah, and he would be safe from her then.

But if he did that then what would happen to all his other plans, plans for which he had worked so hard and waited so long?

No, he would not shoot her. Not yet. He would follow her carefully in the light of day and gradually wear her down. She was weak now, he knew that. Very, very weak. It would not be too long until he would have her. Of that the Ute was certain. A squaw in her condition could not possibly go very far, and she would be so exhausted that when he found her . . .

Inepegut suddenly realized that the pressure in his head had diminished. When he thought of the white squaw it made the pain in his head go away. He would think of her more. He would think of nothing else but her. Tomorrow when he caught her, he . . .

What was that?

Straining his ears and eyes he stared into the darkness around him. The trunks of the trees stood silent and black against the blacker darkness beyond. Overhead the leaves and needles of the trees swayed gently in the night breeze, blocking out large areas of the star-filled sky with their black bulk.

Inepegut could see nothing, yet now the sound was coming again, faintly and from up the hill. Listening intently he strained forward, unable to understand or comprehend what he was hearing. At first he doubted, but soon he knew there was no doubting, no mistaking. What he was listening to was the crying and fussing of a baby. A very tiny baby.

Occasionally he had heard the crying of mountain lions that some said sounded like crying babies, and for a moment he wondered if perhaps that was what he was listening to. But no, it wasn't. Not unless this was a lion that sounded different from all the others he had ever heard. No, what he was hearing had to be a baby, a human baby.

But where had a baby come from? Could the white squaw have given birth to a baby? Inepegut tried to recall what she had looked like lying in the bottom of the wash after Hoskoots had scalped her. Had she been with child? Had her stomach been swollen with child? He tried to remember but the effort was too great and he gave it up when the pain and pressure in his head returned.

Intermittently the crying continued, now loudly, now softly, now not at all, and through it all Inepegut the Crazy Man rocked back and forth with his head held tightly between his hands.

Occasionally he stopped to listen, hoping that the crying would have gone away, hoping against 'hope that it had stopped. But when it hadn't he returned to his slow and gentle rocking back and forth.

Once the thought came that somehow the white squaw had turned herself into a baby, but he quickly forced that thought out. Such ideas did him no good, no good at all. Besides, he was certain that come daylight he would be able to understand even this mystery. Yet it bothered him that the squaw had somehow gotten herself a baby without his knowing of it. Somehow she had tricked him again, and Inepegut cried as he thought of it.

Later he stopped again to listen. This time he heard nothing, no sound at all broke the silence of the night. Even the wind had stopped, and all nature seemed hushed and poised, waiting . . . waiting . . .

Fearfully Inepegut looked around. What kind of a night was this? When would Tabby come up to give his light? Glancing eastward he could see nothing. The sky was as dark in the east as it was anywhere else. But why was it so quiet? Where were the night sounds, the sounds he was so used to? To Inepegut the night had suddenly become a terrifying time, a thing of blackness full of unthinkable terror.

Groping in the darkness he again took up the rifle. As silently then as possible he crawled in under the spreading branches of an old spruce, where he curled up in a ball in the old needles at the base of the tree.

His eyes were shut tightly and the pain in his head was forgotten in the nameless dread that filled his heart. Inepegut had never known such terror as he now experienced. He could not explain it, nor did he try to. With his new rifle beside him he buried his head in his arms and tried to blot out everything, straining against the trunk of the tree for security while he waited in fear for the coming of the dawn. And his only hope was that it would come quickly.

CHAPTER TWENTY-TWO

The woman, crouching in the darkness above the crumbling cliff, also noticed the silence, the sudden change in the Sanpete night. She had done all she could think of to prepare for daylight and the coming of the Indian. She had fed the baby as well as she was able and now she merely rested while she waited for the sun to rise.

Her thirst was terrible and her whole body was hot with fever, yet still she felt . . . well, she felt good. Somehow she felt calm and serene, confident that all would be well. She knew she was lightheaded, but in spite of that, her thinking seemed clear and to her surprise she found herself enjoying the quiet and solitude of the mountains.

Years before she had learned that the mountains, to be enjoyed, demanded aloneness. To know them completely she had to be alone with them in the midst of their emptiness, and despite the distant but ominous presence of the Ute warrior, the woman now felt completely at peace and completely alone.

In the quiet and the darkness of the mountains her body grew still and her mind became empty, a vast reservoir for the receiving of impressions. The slightest sound was heard or felt instantly. Around her the mountains spread in all their mystery and strangeness, their timelessness, while overhead the sky seemed enormous.

As the woman stared at the vastness of the sky, contemplating the infinite number of stars and the Great Being who had created them for His own wisdom and glory, the woman found herself marveling that He who had done such great things was also aware of her, a tiny speck on a world that was itself a tiny speck among the glorious celestial orbs she now beheld. It was truly difficult to believe that it was so.

Yet she knew it was true, and she knew it, nothing doubting. For so great was the warmth, so great were the peace and serenity that filled her soul as she thought of Him, that she knew they could only have come from God. God, who cared enough that He could love even such a one as her. It was more than she could comprehend, and had she tried she would never have been able to explain to another how she felt. Yet her feelings were real enough. In fact her feelings were so strong and so powerful that in the midst of her suffering she found herself, surprisingly, giving thanks to her Heavenly Father for the great blessings she had received at His hand. Jens had been so right when he bore testimony of these truths, these truths that she was just now beginning to feel.

For a long time the woman reclined against the rocks above the edge of the crumbling cliff. She knew how weak she was, and she understood that unless she had water she would probably be dead within a few hours and maybe sooner. Her light-headedness and her almost complete inability to move were certain indications that such was true.

She tried to worry. She forced herself to gaze at the sleeping child and consider what would happen to it if she perished there on the mountain.

All her sense and all her reason told her that she was in desperate trouble, that if she didn't do something quickly it would be forever too late to do anything at all. Both she and the baby would perish. Or worse yet, she would perish and the baby would be taken by the Indians and raised as one of them.

These thoughts were certainly not pleasant, but somehow she could not convince herself that she really had to worry about them. She simply felt too good, too happy to worry. Why, hadn't she been promised that all would work out for the best? Hadn't Jens told her she need only do all she could, and hadn't God Himself given her this sweet feeling of peace during her prayer to Him? Would God have done that if He intended to abandon her at the moment of crisis?

No, He would not. Somehow she knew that and took comfort from it. How He would help her, she didn't know. How He would provide water, or otherwise sustain both she and the baby, was still a mystery. Yet somehow He *would* do it. She knew that and so was simply unable to worry. Worrying would do no good anyway, and as Jens had once said, worrying would only show a lack of faith. That she would not do.

So she sat in the solitude and the stillness of the night, her baby sleeping quietly beside her, and she waited, quietly waited with no doubt in her heart at all.

Thus it was that she noticed the stillness, the sudden cessation of the night sounds around her. Suddenly all nature seemed hushed and waiting, waiting with her.

Finally, at first barely audible but quickly growing in intensity, a fresh wind lashed through the pines and the aspen high above her on the mountain. In the beginning she heard only the sigh, but as it whipped across the ridges and howled down the canyons it grew in volume and intensity until she too was enveloped in its awesome breath.

Holding the child close to her now the woman watched in wonder as black clouds, blacker even than the sky beyond them, scudded across the mountain from the west and quickly obscured the tiny lanterns of the stars.

Thunder growled ominously in the distance and the wind whipped at her bonnet and her skirts and tore at the trees and grass around her. Suddenly the darkness of the night was shattered into a thousand pieces as a stabbing fork of lightning smashed into the hillside not a quarter of a mile away, momentarily blinding her with the brilliancy of its flash. Forever the jagged streak seemed to quiver in the night as its single tentacle groped about the slope for a permanent hold. But then suddenly it failed in its search and was gone, leaving nothing but the smell of brimstone and its image burned into the woman's numbed vision.

Instantly then her senses reeled and she cowered on the shaking earth as the thunder, a tremendous explosion of celestial power, tore with amazing weight at the tattered threads of her consciousness, growling and battering endlessly as it rumbled back and forth across the narrow valley.

Nor was the sound dead yet when the rains came, a few splattering drops sent ahead to feel the way and then slashing sheets of water that came tearing down the mountainside before the fury of the winds. Great slashing sheets that soaked and inundated all before them as they swept down the long hills and out into the valley of Sanpete.

Finally the full fury of the storm hit the mountain valley. Lightning flashed continuously until the night seemed almost as day, and the booming and the growling of the thunder were one long and never ending nerve-tingling cacophony of sound. The rain fell in torrents, and almost instantly tiny trickles began seeking the low places to form rivulets. These in turn, bearing their burden of sticks, mud, and silt, coursed down the slopes to sweep with ever growing power along the draws and into the washes, ravines, and arroyos of the valley floor, there to ultimately lose themselves in the parched and dry earth that eagerly awaited their arrival.

The woman, high on the slope, lay on her back with her arms outstretched, eyes shut tightly and her mouth open to the sweetness and deliciousness of the driving rain. The baby, secure under a nearby rocky overhang, slept peacefully on while the woman lay in the mud and considered in awe the power and fury of the sudden summer storm. The storm that had swept so quickly down the mountainside to provide the water she had prayed for and so desperately needed to save the life of her baby.

And as the rain swept across her tired and tortured body, caressing her aching limbs with its wet and somehow gentle tenderness, the woman wept and again gave thanks to God, the Eternal Father whom she had so recently learned of. She gave thanks that He was kind and forgiving enough to answer the prayer of one as sinful as she had been. For now she could save her baby, now she could fulfill Jens's dying admonition and save the life of their tiny child. How she would do it she knew not. She knew only that it would be so, and her soul rejoiced with the knowledge.

The storm, one typical of the mountains, was of short duration. By the time the sky was ready to begin graying in the east it was not only over but most of the clouds had vanished from the sky.

The woman, having slacked her thirst from a small pool in the rock, breathed deeply of the pure fresh air. Nothing, she thought, smelled so good as clean mountain air directly following a storm. She then picked up the baby to commence her flight when a sudden thought seized her.

Once before, so long ago it seemed, she had turned away an Indian by speaking in his own tongue. Her knowledge of the Ute language was sketchy at best, yet it might be worth a try. Actually, she didn't even know if the Ute were still out there, or even if he still pursued her. But she felt that he did, and she thought too that he was within hearing distance. So what could she lose by trying?

Moving away from the cliff she turned so she would be speaking

up into the mountain. Her father had once told her this would help
to hide where she really was by bouncing her voice around somewhat.

When she opened her mouth to yell she was surprised that no
sound came out, and it took several efforts before she could speak
with any degree of steadiness at all in her voice. Finally, though, she
was ready, and slowly she began to shout.

"Ayaii!"

"Ayaii katz-ne-ate towats, katz-te-suah katz-ne-ate towats! Ick-in-
ish pi-equey-band. Pi-equey-band . . ."

Here she paused, unable to think of the word she wanted. Finally
in desperation she shouted it in English.

"Pi-equey-band or else em e-iqueay. Te-we-ne em katz-te-suah
nam-i-peds, or else a squaw will puck-ki em and lul-nel-ka em quan-
na tabby. Pi-equey-band inepegut nan-i-peds, before em-e-iqueay!
Ick-in-ish em inepegut . . . ah, if you don't!"

Again the woman turned to stare out into the predawn darkness,
listening for some sound, some reply to her orders. Truthfully she
was not even certain that what she had shouted made sense, but it
was the best she could do. If the Ute had heard her and then understood her, perhaps he would do as she had told him. But she knew
that the chance of that was slim, so slim that she must not count on
it at all.

The hill was slippery with mud and so the woman was forced to
move slowly and with great caution. It was still dark, though a trace
of light could be seen across the valley to the east. She glanced longingly at it, wishing that the sun would appear to warm her up and
dry her clothing out. For now in addition to her other problems she
was shaking with the cold. Partially it was her own fault, for inad-
vertently she had allowed the blanket to get wet in the storm. Now it
gave little protection from the cold but seemed to the woman just an
added weight, something extra to carry. She considered discarding it
but didn't have the energy to do so, and after that one thought it
never crossed her mind again.

It was impossible to hide her tracks as she slipped and slid
through the muddy darkness, and the woman quickly realized that
she was simply not able to climb higher on the slope or even to hold
a course roughly parallel to the level of the valley. She was slowly
descending the side of the mountain because of her weakness.

And she was weak! Never in her life had she felt so weak. Her legs felt like green willow wands, and over and over she fell to the ground, clutching the child tightly so she would not be injured.

Once when she fell she slid and rolled at least a dozen feet down the rocky hill before slamming into the trunk of a tree. The impact knocked her breath away and for a moment or two she was sure she would die right there.

Then she thought of the baby. Where was the baby? Desperately she looked around. How could she have dropped the baby? But there she was, back up the slope where she had first fallen.

In an agony of fear she clawed her way back up the hill to where she had dropped the screaming baby, desperately afraid that the child had been injured in the fall. But no, with a little love and a bit of song for comfort the child was quickly asleep again, secure in the arms of her appointed mother.

But now the woman realized that she must make a decision. If she hadn't dropped the baby she might have been killed, crushed between her body and the tree. She had stayed on the hillside because she hoped in the daylight it would enable her to see the Indian who followed her. She could possibly continue along the slope for some time yet, but the effort was sapping her strength rapidly and it was becoming increasingly dangerous for both her and the baby.

Her only alternative was to angle down the steep hill and across the rolling foothills to the valley floor, where the going would be both easier and safer, but where it would also be easier for the Ute to find her and surprise her.

That thought alone terrified her, but she realized that her main desire, her only desire, must be to save the life of her daughter. To do that she must make it to Uinta Springs and to help.

Accordingly, in the gray light of dawn she began moving down the slope toward the gently rolling hills of Sanpete Valley. Where possible she did her best to avoid leaving a distinct trail, and occasionally she tore another strip of cloth from her clothing and left it tied to the top of a bush along her way, hoping against hope that it might accomplish something worthwhile.

As the sun's first rays topped the hills to the east and fell on the woman they revealed a strange sight, a sort of stumbling caricature of a human being dragging a slimy object through the mud of the valley. The old quilt, wet, torn, and covered with mud, hung loosely from her shoulders to drag in the mud at her feet. Her skirt and blouse, or what remained of them, were so mud-covered that they appeared to be the same garment. Her bonnet, plastered to her head with dried and drying blood, flopped its brim down over her face with each stumbling step she took. Even the blanket in which her thin arms held the baby was covered with drying mud. Her eyes, dark and hollow, peered out from a face so gaunt and thin that even Jens, had he been there to see her, would not have recognized her.

On and on she walked, stumbling, falling, crawling, rolling, climbing, falling; falling and falling again. She did not know when she came down off the mountain, she had no concept of stumbling through muddy ravines or crawling up sandy and rock-strewn slopes. Even the occasional strips of cloth she tied on bushes became a reflex action, nothing more.

Sometime in the morning the baby started crying, and a little later the woman looked down and realized with a start that somehow the child had found her breast and was nursing, nursing contentedly as she stumbled down the rocky bed of an old wash.

Twice during the early hours of morning the woman stopped to drink out of pools of rainwater. But quickly the sun grew hot, the ground dried out, and soon damp and cracking mudholes were all that remained from the storm of the night before.

Onward and ever onward the woman struggled, pulling herself and the baby across the low rolling hills and along the rock-strewn ravines. Her hands and knees were torn and bloody, her muscles cramped in agonizing protest at the abuse she was giving them, her vision blurred and swam before her, and her mind, her keen and active mind, grew numb in the heat of the sun.

Her mouth was like cotton, she could not feel her tongue, and she no longer even knew whether she was crawling or walking. Somehow it did not seem to matter anymore. Nothing mattered anymore. Nothing except that she keep on moving, keep moving toward that non-existent and ever retreating place called Uinta Springs.

How far away could it possibly be? It seemed to her dazed and groggy mind that she had walked all day, that she had walked all her life, yet somehow the sun said it was still morning. How could that be possible? How could that . . .

Her head was a hollow drum, and something was beating inside it, on and on and on . . .

"O dear God, how much farther will I have to go . . . ?"

Again the woman cast her vision upward, and as she did so movement caught her attention, a movement that took a moment or two to identify. In the air, circling above her, was a buzzard, a solitary buzzard winging back and forth in the morning sky, back and forth, back and forth . . .

"Jens, help me . . . please . . ."

CHAPTER TWENTY-THREE

The valley was still and the sun was hot. There under the tree, now that the breeze had died, it was sticky and still. The air was sultry from the rain the night before, and sweat trickled down the woman's face. Her neck itched from juniper needles and dust picked up when she rolled partly over, and around her was only the silence of the morning.

Awareness came then and the woman suddenly realized that she had been unconscious. She had lost consciousness! But for how long? Where was the sun? More important, where was the baby? Had the Indian come and taken the baby?

Desperately she struggled to roll over, to roll over and sit up. But she couldn't. The effort was too great and she fell back exhausted, unable to even see if the baby were near her. Her eyes! Her eyes felt as though they were on fire they burned so badly, and for some reason she couldn't get them open.

Pray, she thought. Pray for strength! But even that seemed beyond her. Her tongue was a wooden stick protruding from the gaping hole that was her mouth, and the lips that surrounded it were cracked and dry. No matter how she tried she could not make her mouth work. It just would not form her fragmented thoughts into words.

But the spinning was the worst thing. She was spinning again and it felt as though she was forever falling and there was nothing to hang on to. It was so dark . . . so dark . . . How she wanted to scream, to cry for help . . . to cry . . .

"Dear God," she pleaded mentally as she spun deeper and deeper into the hole of unconsciousness.

"O dear God . . ."

But it was no use, no use, and she was going down deeper . . . deeper . . .

"Voman."

The voice was calm and quiet, so quiet that again she almost did not hear it. Yet weakly she grasped at the hope she had in her husband, grasping for the only thing that she had left to grasp.

"Jens," she croaked in a whisper, struggling again to sit up and open her eyes.

"Jens? I . . . can't find the baby . . . Where is the baby?"

"Hush, voman. Yust reach out your hand und you vill find the child. She is fine, und you need not vorry about her."

"Jens, where are you? I can't see you . . ."

"I am here, voman. but that is not important now. Yust reach out und you vill hold the baby."

Blindly the woman reached out, groping in the darkness of the sunlit morning for her baby, groping for the tiny child that she had promised to save and preserve.

And then she found her, still wrapped in her blanket and still sleeping soundly. Quickly she felt beneath the blanket, feeling with her mutilated hand to see that the baby was all right. Yes, her breath was coming at regular intervals and her heartbeat was strong. The baby was well.

Relieved, the woman relaxed in the shade of the juniper. It felt so good to just be still, to lie down and know that she and the baby were safe, safe because Jens was there. She was so glad that Jens was finally back, that he . . .

"Jens . . . Jens!"

Again she struggled to sit up, to open the hollow pits of fire that had once been her eyes.

"Jens! Don't leave us . . . Please don't go away . . ."

At last her eyes opened, but everything was so blurry, so misty and indistinct. But where was Jens? Desperately she looked around for her husband, her husband who only a moment before had spoken to her. Surely he would not leave her now . . . Surely . . .

But all she could see through her blurry vision was the sky, the earth, the rocks, sage, and junipers.

She was alone! Except for the baby she was alone.

The baby! She had to save the baby, to get her to Uinta Springs and to safety. Why was she lying in the shade resting when she had so far to go, so far to go to get the baby to the safety of Uinta Springs? The child surely was a good baby, no fussing or carrying on as she might have done. Why, her youngest brother, when he was a baby, had never stopped crying. He . . .

The woman was deep down, down in a black hole struggling to

crawl out. On and on she crawled, up and up she climbed, always moving and never seeming to move. But way above, far far away, she could see an opening, a beautiful patch of light that . . .

Somehow she could see out, somehow she could see out of the hole and into a beautiful valley, a beautiful little valley with lush meadows lining a winding stream. Oh to have a drink from that stream! If only she could crawl up to the edge of the darkness that held her a prisoner.

But it was so far away, so very far away, so very far . . . and it was hard to crawl, harder than anything she had ever done in her life. She would never get out, never . . .

The woman tried to roll over and once again she felt the itching of juniper needles on her face and arms. Was she still beneath the tree? Somehow it seemed to the woman that she had been there for days, endless days of struggling to get up and carry the baby to safety. But now her eyes were open and she could see the baby lying quietly beside her. Incredibly the child was asleep.

With a herculean effort the woman willed her hands and arms to go to the baby, to pick her up and hold her close to her. Then she stumbled awkwardly to her feet. She knew she had to start walking, but her legs felt like sticks propped up under her and somehow they would not do what she willed them to do. It was exactly as if they were part of another person, exactly as if . . .

What was that? Across the wash she saw movement, something moving in the brush. Desperately, the woman strained her eyes, trying to clear her vision, to see if . . .

Jens? Could that be Jens over there?

Again the brush moved, and slowly the form of a man materialized from the blur of her vision, a man carrying something in his hand.

Through straining eyes she struggled to see who it was, to see if it was Jens come back to help her, to . . .

The Indian! Suddenly the woman realized that it was the naked savage who was standing there not thirty feet away. It was the Ute, and he was smiling—no, he was laughing, laughing loudly as he stood there watching her. But somehow he had changed . . . something was wrong with his face. It was all puffy, it was all puffy and bloody.

And as suddenly as that the woman realized that she had lost. With all her efforts she had finally been run down and now her baby, her beautiful little daughter that Jens had thought so much of, was at the mercy of the Indian.

Haltingly she took a step toward him, her baby clutched in one bloody hand while the other was outstretched pleadingly toward the Indian.

Instantly his laughter vanished and with a savage curse he threw his rifle to his shoulder, took careful aim, and fired.

There was a tremendous explosion and the woman felt herself falling, falling . . . Into the black hole . . . past the pretty little valley . . . past Jens . . . past . . .

CHAPTER TWENTY-FOUR

For Inepegut the whole time of darkness was one long nightmare of horror. His head hurt terribly and the wound on his leg was now stinging badly. Then add to that the terrors of the storm. Rainstorms he was used to, but that particular storm had terrified him, for lightning had struck very close to him several times and the acrid smell of brimstone still burned in his nostrils.

But even that would have been livable if it hadn't been for what the white squaw had done, or rather what she had said. For somehow that squaw, that white squaw who was so nearly dead, had spoken to him in his own tongue. Worse yet, and what almost made him abandon the search, was that somehow she had learned his name and had used it, not once but twice. Just as Hoskoots had done! If he hadn't intended killing her before, that certainly sealed her doom, for she must not know of his identity. That gave her too much power over him.

But the thing she had said, it was so strange that even now he could recall it word for terrifying word.

"Ayaii," she had shouted.

"Ayaii, no name man, foolish no name man! I say go home. Go home . . .

"Go home . . . you die! Make haste, foolish old man . . . squaw will kill you and leave you to stink in the sun!

"Go home, crazy old man! Make haste before you die! I call you Crazy Man . . ."

And then she was silent and she was gone. But how could she have learned his name, how could she have learned who followed her and where he was?

Inepegut had been so surprised that he had raised his rifle to fire at the voice in the darkness, but the sound seemed to come from everywhere and at last he gave it up in confusion. He must wait for Tabby-moushy, he must wait for sunrise.

In the gray light of dawn he had come out of the thicket of spruce and aspen to kill the woman, but as he passed the sapling with the knife still tied to the top of it he shuddered and turned away. She was indeed a hard person to kill.

The rain had washed out any sign the squaw might have left, but at last he was learning to know how she thought. When he saw the cliff he knew almost instinctively that she had climbed its face, and so he began to climb it too.

The crumbling rock was slippery and wet from the rain and that alone saved his life. For the squaw had set a deadfall, a huge boulder held in place with a small stick that he almost certainly would bump as he climbed past it.

And so he did, but he was even then slipping on the slick face of the cliff and sliding out of the path of the crashing boulder. Still it smashed him a wicked blow on the side of his face as it swept past.

For a long time a very painful and shaking Inepegut clung to the face of the cliff, but at last his anger at the squaw returned and with it a little of his courage. Forcing himself to the top of the cliff he began to sort out the sign of the woman, the woman and the baby. For there was no doubt about it now. The woman had somehow gotten a baby, and she was carrying it with her. Well, no matter. It would only slow her down more. In a matter of moments Inepegut was following the wide-open trail left on the muddy slope of the mountain.

Inepegut spent little time thinking as he ran, for if he did he found he could think only of the pain of his head and his wounds. So he simply closed his mind and ran.

When the trail turned to descend the mountain Inepegut paused to give thought, but then satisfied he followed on, confident now that her weakness was growing ever greater.

But then he came to the first bush with the white rag tied to the top and it stopped him completely. He wanted badly to see if she had left another arrow, but even more badly he wanted to avoid further injury from the squaw's devilish traps.

For long moments he debated, but at last he gave it up as hopeless and began working his way slowly and carefully in a large half circle around the bush. He was taking too much time and care, but when at last he came unscathed to her trail again he felt certain that the loss of time had been worth the effort.

Several times during the morning he encountered the same situation, and each time he handled it exactly the same way as he had the time before. He was fairly certain that there weren't traps near each flag, but then what if there were? So he lost much time and stayed alive, and what matter was a little more time?

The squaw was very weak and everwhere along her trail there were signs of it. At times she crawled more than she walked, and when she walked it was with such stumbling and staggering that Inepegut was amazed that she could continue. It was more than he had seen anyone ever do, and he could not imagine that such an effort was possible.

Still she moved ahead and Inepegut carefully followed, ever following her trail and ever searching ahead for some sign of the squaw.

Yet even with this constant vigil he almost missed her, she was so well camouflaged with the dirty quilt. If she hadn't moved, trying to roll over, he would have gone right by her, circling a rag she had tied in a bush.

But now he saw her lying beneath a juniper and his heart leaped within him. Instantly he dropped to the earth and began worming his way forward. He was taking no chances. She was not going to get away again. Not after all the trouble he had had getting her.

Oo-ah, what was she doing now? She was sitting up . . . no . . . she was slowly standing up! Had she seen him? Was she foolish enough to try and escape again?

No! He would not let her get away! Instantly he jumped to his feet to show himself to her, to frighten her into submission.

Oo-ah, it was working, it was working! She was standing still, afraid to move, afraid of the great Inepegut.

This was fine, this was very fine. It had been a long chase, but now he knew it had been worth it. At last he could do with her as he chose. At last he could . . .

And then he laughed, loudly and merrily he laughed as he thought of all he was going to do with her, thinking . . .

What was she doing? *What was she doing?* She was walking, trying again to get away. She was coming toward him, staring at him, raising her hand at him . . .

He must stop her! He could not let her hurt him again!

Kill her! Kill her with the rifle! It was safe, and he could do it from here easily. Quickly, before she . . .

Instantly the rifle was at his shoulder and he was viewing the bloody and dirty face of the woman across the bead at the end of the barrel.

For an instant he wavered, wondering, but then his decision was made and he steadied his aim on the woman, the white squaw he had wanted so badly, and gently he squeezed the trigger.

There was a terrific explosion, an immense cloud of white smoke, and the body of the woman, the baby clutched tightly in her arms, turned a little and finally toppled quietly to the earth.

Slowly the smoke from the rifle dissipated and drifted away, and then the valley was silent, silent save for the wind as it drifted through the brush and trees and down the long hills of Sanpete Valley, Territory of Utah.

CHAPTER TWENTY-FIVE

"Pa, did you just hear something?"

"Like what, son?"

"I dunno. I thought maybe I heard a gunshot, but I couldn't be sure."

"Nope! I didn't hear anything like that. And to tell the truth I surely hope you didn't either. I surely hope so."

"How come, Pa?"

"Because your ma told me this morning when we left home to watch out careful for you and to keep you out of trouble while we were in Nephi. And son, if there's one thing I've learned living here in Sanpete, it's that a gunshot where there hadn't ought to be a gunshot most generally means trouble, trouble with a capital T."

For a few moments the two rode in silence while the boy considered what his father had said.

They had left Fort Ephraim long before daylight and had ridden hard until they arrived at Uinta Springs, a favorite camping place for weary travelers on the trail through the northern end of Sanpete Valley. Here they had rested for an hour, eating a hearty breakfast while their horses watered in the stream and fed on the lush meadow grass.

Frequently when they stopped here they found others, generally Scandinavian emigrants on their way south to new homes and new dreams.

But today the springs were empty and the two found themselves alone. Yet they minded neither the quiet nor the solitude, and the father wisely used the time drawing near to his son, who was himself drawing nigh to manhood.

Following breakfast they cleaned up, mounted their horses, and rode northward across the gentle rolling and sage-covered hills that led into Salt Creek Canyon. From Uinta Springs it was just fifteen miles through the canyon to Nephi, and if they rode carefully they should make it easily by early afternoon.

"Pa, there must have been quite a storm here last night, don'tcha reckon?"

"Yep. I've been noticing that myself. Look at how the mud keeps balling up on the horses' hooves. We'd best watch that and not let it get too heavy. Last thing we need in this canyon is a lame horse."

"Do you reckon I could've heard a gun?"

"Oh, I expect so, though I don't know who'd fire it out here. Not unless it was Injuns."

"You think they might be hunting?"

"Could be, son Could be."

"Sunday the bishop said we could work on our crops this summer without fear, Pa. He said Brother Brigham had made certain we would have peace with the Utes from now on. That is, we will have peace if we can whip Johnston's army."

The man looked carefully at his son, waiting until he had his attention before he spoke.

"Boy, when you talk of President Young you call him President Young. You hear? You have neither the years nor the right to be so familiar as to call him Brother Brigham."

"But Pa . . ."

"No arguments, boy. He's the Prophet and you talk of him with respect. You hear me?"

"Yes, Pa. Whatever you say."

"Good. Now about them Injuns. What the bishop said is right. We are at peace with them, or at least we are supposed to be. But son, you've got to understand that Injuns are notional critters. There's just no telling what they'll do. One day they'll promise you an alliance of peace, and the next day the very same Injuns will lift your scalp."

"But why, Pa? If they've given their word on it, why don't they keep it?"

"That's a fair question, son. Folks've been pondering that for quite a spell, and usually without coming up with any good answer. But if you ask me, I'd say it was because the Injuns just don't think like we do."

"Huh? I don't get it."

"Well, son, the way I see it, most folks assume the Injuns have Christian values and virtues. That just isn't so. At least not yet. Their philosophy of life is war . . . to them peace is unrealistic. The better thief a man is the more honored he becomes among his people. If he can kill an enemy he is a real hero. And never you mind about how he does it. According to them the more sneaky he is in doing it the better. There's none of this brotherly love and turn the other cheek stuff for an Injun. They still live pretty much under an eye-for-an-eye law, only they carry it way to the extreme.

"That's why I call them notional. They take a notion to stealing something, they steal it. They take a notion to killing someone, they kill him. It's a simple law, easy to remember. But it sure raises hob with white folks trying to build up a country. It's downright difficult getting some folks to stay with Injuns running around killing all their neighbors."

"How'd you learn all this, Pa?"

"Oh, just by studying them and watching them."

"When've you done that?"

"Here and there most all my life, son. I learned young it pays to keep your eyes open, your mouth shut, and your memory in gear. You're pretty good at that too, boy, so keep it up. That and asking questions . . ."

He grinned then and the boy grinned back, happy that he was old enough to talk with his father man to man.

For a time they rode in silence, each absorbed in his own thoughts, each enjoying the presence of the other without feeling the need for constant chatter. Finally, though, the older man broke the silence.

"You notice anything unusual, son?"

"No . . . Not unless you mean the buzzard."

"What's unusual about a buzzard, boy?"

The boy looked carefully at his father, uncertain if he was funning him or not. But he looked serious enough, so the boy answered.

"It ain't the buzzard so much, Pa. It's more what it's doing that strikes me as unusual."

"How's that?"

"Well, mostly buzzards circle a lot, just like that one's doing. Only in their circles they slip up and down the valley, covering a lot of country.

"But not that one there. I've been watching it for maybe five minutes now, and as near as I can tell, that buzzard hasn't gone anywhere. I figure he's got something spotted and he's just waiting for the right moment to drop on down. To me he acts nervous or something."

The man looked approvingly at his son.

"You'll do, son. You'll do. Do you want to ride over and investigate?"

"I dunno, Pa. I've been thinking of that gunshot I thought I heard earlier. Could be there's someone needs help over there. If there was it would surely be a shame if we was to ride on by. Don't you think so?"

"Yep. Reckon I do."

"Pa?"

"Uh-huh?"

"You got your rifle loaded?"

At this the older man laughed outright, holding his rifle up so the boy could see for himself that it was. Quickly, though, he became serious again.

"Son, we could just ride over there like we're riding now, or we could split up in case there's someone wants to make a target out of us. Which do you think we should do?"

"Let's split up."

"Fine. You ride straight on in, only go slowly. I'll circle around and come on in from the other side. If you see anything suspicious at all don't be afraid to kick that horse and skedaddle, and fire a shot so I'll know you got trouble. You ready?"

"I reckon so."

With that the man wheeled his horse and rode rapidly away, leaving his son alone in the stillness of the valley.

Shading his eyes the boy looked up at the buzzard. It had climbed higher into the air, but it was still circling above the same place. Again the boy wondered what it could see. How he envied a bird's ability to fly, to float along as free as the wind and nearly as fast. That would be such great fun to soar along up there, riding the winds and drifting through the clouds, carefully watching all below . . .

His father was nearly opposite from him now, so the boy kicked his horse slowly forward. He held his rifle ready with both hands, letting his horse pick its own way, and his eyes were constantly moving, constantly searching for any indication of danger. The horse walked slowly as it skirted clumps of sage and skirted a ravine looking for the easiest path down through it. Then with a snort and a shake of its head, it stepped down and across, then lunged up the far side.

For a quarter of a mile the boy rode forward, always alert but seeing nothing. Again he looked up. The buzzard was directly above him now, still circling, and his father was only fifty yards off and drawing closer.

Still he could see nothing. Everything looked just as it should look. But now he was getting jumpy. His mouth was dry and his hands were sweaty, and suddenly he wished his father was beside him instead of so far away. This was scary, more scary even than . . .

Suddenly his horse snorted and reared back. The boy, fighting for control of the animal, at first saw nothing. But then when he did he was momentarily terrified himself and pulled the animal back even farther.

Something, some shapeless something, was struggling on the ground over by that old juniper.

"Pa . . . *Pa, come quick!* There's something here!"

The boy then dismounted and holding his rifle ready he walked cautiously forward, certain only that he had never seen anything like this before. The thing, whatever it was, was creeping slowly along the ground, pausing, flopping flat, and then rising to move forward again, though very slowly.

Slowly, very slowly he advanced until he was just a few feet away, and now he was certain that he was looking upon a human being, a filthy human being completely covered by a dirty brown quilt. It must be an old Indian.

Picking up a long stick he reached out and flipped the blanket up and over, and to his amazement he beheld the gaunt and filthy form of a woman, a *white woman*.

"Pa, Pa . . . Come'r quick!"

"Yes, son. I'm here, and I see her. Get your canteen while I turn her over. There. Now take it easy, ma'am, take it . . ."

"Oh my dear God in Heaven! Son! Hurry with that water! This woman has a baby here, and they both look to be in a bad way."

Quickly the man worked, washing her face and forcing a little liquid between her parched and cracked lips while his son stood anxiously but helplessly by.

"Pa, she sure has got a lot of blood on her bonnet."

"Yes she does. I reckon she's been scalped."

"Scalped? But I thought you died if you got scalped."

"Normally you do, son, but I've known of a few who've gone for years with bare skull showing on the top of their heads. This woman, though. She's about done. Look at her hands and knees. She's come a long way, a powerful long way."

"Is the baby all right?"

"Yes, but it seems to be asleep. She's got ahold of it so tight I can't get it away from her."

"Do you reckon its hers?"

"Can't tell. She looks old, though. Powerful old to have a baby this tiny. So I'd guess it wasn't. Still, there's no way of knowing for sure, not unless we can revive her and ask her."

The man hesitated, and then spoke again.

"Son, get on your horse and work a ways down her backtrail, and do it careful. Let me know if you find anything."

The boy backed away and mounting up he rode off. As soon as he was away the man quickly but carefully examined the woman's emaciated body for further injury. She had been shot once, in the head, and then she had been scalped. Finding no other wounds, however, he covered her again with what clothing she had left and then draped the old quilt around her.

After forcing more water down her throat he gently but firmly pried her arm from around the baby, which he then placed carefully on the ground beside her. He then began rubbing her arms and legs, striving to stimulate circulation.

Suddenly her eyes fluttered open and she struggled to sit up. "Jens?" she croaked in a hoarse whisper. "Jens, wait . . . for me . . . please . . . I've almost . . . got her there . . . Like I . . . promised . . ."

"Ma'am, you just take it easy and lay back . . ."

"Jens, come closer . . . come closer . . . If you'll help me . . . I can get . . . into . . . the valley . . . I can get out . . . of this . . . hole . . . and into your valley . . . with you . . ."

"Ma'am, who's this Jens? There's nobody here but me, ma'am, me and my son . . ."

"Jens Jergensen," she almost shouted, "you said you'd wait! Come back for me . . . please . . . the valley . . . baby . . ."

The woman relaxed and the man trickled more water down her throat. Jens Jergensen. Who could that be? Could be he was her husband, but if so, where was he? The old woman was obviously delirious, obviously . . .

"Who are you?"

The question was calm, quiet, and the man, startled, gazed down into the clear eyes of the woman.

"Why . . . uh . . . I'm Brother Pederson, ma'am. Jacob Pederson. And that's my boy yonder on the horse. He's the one that found you."

"Is the baby well? Can you care for it?"

"It's fit as a fiddle, ma'am. And me and the boy can surely take you both home with us. But who are you, ma'am?"

For a moment she looked up at him in silence, but then a trace of a smile flashed across her face and she calmly replied.

"My husband is Jens Jergensen, he who gave his life for me. And I, my name is . . . is Mrs. Jens Jergensen."

"Ma'am, is the baby yours? Ma'am?"

But the woman was looking off, staring past him and no longer listening to his questions.

"Jens . . . I'm so glad you came back . . . And Kjersta too . . . It's so nice to . . . What's that? No, of course I didn't . . . not ever . . . Jens, she's safe now . . . just like you asked . . . Yes, I know it's true . . . here is my hand . . . I love . . ."

"Pa," the boy whispered after a long moment, "is she dead?"

"Yes, son. She's dead."

"Who was she talking to just now? Did she think your name was Jens?"

"No, I don't reckon she did. There was somebody else here, son, somebody else here to meet her."

"Honest?"

"Son, this woman's husband came for her. As sure as I'm sitting here holding her he did. That's real, and I want you to write it down in your memory and don't you ever forget it. Do you hear me?"

"Well sure, Pa, I hear you. Only . . ."

"No more questions, son. You think about this and we'll talk about it another time. Now you take the baby and mount up while I put Mrs. Jergensen's body up on my horse. It's a far piece to Fort Ephraim and we'd best be moving."

"But what about the others, Pa? Don't you think we ought to check and see if there are any others?"

"Not now, son. If there are any others left alive they'll make it back to Nephi. Right now our big problem is to get this child home where your ma can look after it. That's the first life we've got to save. I reckon it's dirty and plenty hungry, too, and your ma's the

best one I know to take care of that. Then we'll come back tomorrow
to see what else we can find. We'll bring others too, just in case."

"Pa?"

"Yes."

"Is this here baby a boy or a girl?"

"I don't know, son. I never looked."

"Pa, wouldn't it be funny if it was a girl and we got to keep her?"

The man remained silent and the boy did not see him wipe the
tears from his eyes.

"I don't mean funny really. But Pa, it sure would be something, us
burying our baby sister one week and finding another baby sister the
next week."

"Yes, son, it surely would be something. It surely would at that."

South they went then, south through the rocks and sage of Sanpete
Valley, the boy carrying the baby gently in his arms while his father
carefully kept the body of the old woman in his saddle.

The air was still and warm and the valley was silent. Nothing
moved in the heat of the afternoon, nothing but an old buzzard that
spun in ever narrowing and ever lowering circles in the air behind
the two riders. For the buzzard it had been a long wait . . . almost
too long . . .

"Pa, I almost forgot to tell you."

"What was that?"

"Back there when you sent me to follow her trail? Well, I found
something back there, Pa. I found a rifle, all blowed to bits and still
smoking."

"Anything else?"

"Well, there was a sight of blood on the ground, still sticky, and
some blood and funny tracks leading off into the cedars, like whoever made them was hurt bad and was crawling."

"Did you follow them, son?"

"Not far. I had a bad feeling about it, so came back."

For a moment they were both silent, and then the boy spoke
again.

"Pa, I figure whoever fired that rifle was after this woman, was trying to kill her. But somewhere he got dirt jammed in the muzzle of
his rifle and didn't know about it. Then when he pulled the trigger it
blew up in his face, about doing him in. At least I figure it did, with
all that blood around there. Anyway, I've been thinking, Pa, and I'll
bet that's the shot I thought I heard earlier. Don'tcha think?"

"It probably was, all right. What did you do with the rifle?"

"Nothing. I was figuring on going back."

"Well, that's fine. We can look for the man then too. If he's still alive we'll do what we can. If he's dead, tomorrow ought to be soon enough to bury him. Right now the most important thing we can do is get this little child home to your ma, before it dies too. Your ma'll surely be het up about this youngen when she sees it. I can't hardly wait to see her face light up, replacing all those tears we've been seeing. Com'on boy, let's ride!"

"I'm with you, Pa, all the way."